Dearest

Camfield Novels of Love mark a very exciting era of my books with Jove. They have already published nearly two hundred of my titles since they became my first publisher in America, and now all my original paperback romances in the future will be published exclusively by them.

As you already know, Camfield Place in Hertfordshire is my home, which originally existed in 1275, but was rebuilt in 1867 by the grandfather of Beatrix Potter.

It was here in this lovely house, with the best view in the county, that she wrote *The Tale of Peter Rabbit*. Mr. McGregor's garden is exactly as she described it. The door in the wall that the fat little rabbit could not squeeze underneath and the goldfish pool where the white cat sat twitching its tail are still there.

I had Camfield Place blessed when I came here in 1950 and was so happy with my husband until he died, and now with my children and grandchildren, that I know the atmosphere is filled with love and we have all been very lucky.

It is easy here to write of love and I know you will enjoy the Camfield Novels of Love. Their plots are definitely exciting and the covers very romantic. They come to you, like all my books, with love.

Bless you,

Barbara Cartland

A New Camfield Novel of Love by
Barbara Cartland

Saved by Love

JOVE BOOKS, NEW YORK

SAVED BY LOVE

A Jove Book/published by arrangement with
the author

PRINTING HISTORY
Jove edition/November 1988

ISBN: 0-515-09804-3

Jove Books are published by The Berkley Publishing Group,
200 Madison Avenue, New York, New York 10016.
The name "JOVE" and the "J" logo
are trademarks belonging to Jove Publications, Inc.

PRINTED IN THE UNITED STATES OF AMERICA

10 9 8 7 6 5 4 3 2 1

chapter one

1865

LADY Yursa Holme was humming a little tune to herself as she walked back from the garden towards the house.

It was a sunny spring day and she was thinking that nothing could be more lovely than the daffodils making a golden carpet under the trees.

As she turned the corner she saw the lovely Queen Anne house where the Earls of Holme and Lisgood had lived for the last hundred and fifty years.

Outside the front door there was a very smart carriage drawn by two excellent horses.

She recognised both Jem and the old coachman in his tiered coat and cockaded hat sitting on the box.

This meant, she knew, that her grandmother, the Dowager Lady Helmsdale to whom she was devoted, was calling on her father.

1

Ever since she had been a little girl, all the romance in Yursa's life had been supplied by her grandmother, who was half French, telling her stories of the *Ducs* of Burgundy.

Instead of the usual children's fairy-tales of "Cinderella," "Red-Riding-Hood," and "Hansel and Gretel," Yursa had been brought up on the exploits of Philip the Bold, John the Fearless, and Charles the Rash.

They were so much part of her imagination that she dreamed of them at night and was sure when she fell in love it would be with somebody like Philip the Good.

During his fifty-year reign he had achieved one of the most cultured Courts in Europe.

The *Ducs* of Burgundy had not only all fought bravely, but had also summoned the most outstanding artists and writers to their Courts.

They had been revered for their chivalry and kindness of those in need.

As Yursa hurried towards the house, she was wondering if her grandmother had news from France.

Perhaps she had just come on a purely social visit.

She stopped to pat the horses and to ask the old coachman whom she had known since she was a child if his rheumatism was better and if his son was doing well.

He was working in one of the great vineyards of Burgundy and was, Yursa knew, deeply interested in the wines, which all good Burgundians enjoyed as much as they enjoyed fighting.

When the old man had finished a long story of all the troubles and illnesses of his family, she slipped

2

into the house, eager to see her grandmother.

Once in the hall, she took off the shoes in which she had been walking.

So as not to dirty the carpets, she put on the satin slippers which were waiting for her under one of the chairs.

She paused for a moment to tidy her hair in an ancient gold-framed mirror.

Then she hurried towards her father's Study, where she knew she would find him at this time of the day.

Her feet made no sound on the thick carpet, and as she put out her hand towards the Study door she realised it was ajar and she could hear her grandmother's voice.

She was just about to walk in, when she heard her own name.

"It would be the marriage I have always envisaged for Yursa," she heard her grandmother say, "but if we do not hurry to arrange it, we may be too late."

Yursa stood still, surprised and a little frightened by what she had just heard.

"Yursa is not yet eighteen," she heard her father the Earl reply, "and I have already planned that next month I will take her to London, where she will make her curtsy to the Queen."

"I know that is what you intend," the Dowager agreed, "at the same time, as I have just said, we may be too late."

"What do you mean by that?"

There was a short pause, as if the Dowager were thinking what to answer, before she replied:

"I will be frank with you, Edward. I hear that

César is obsessed at the moment with a woman whom all his relatives find totally undesirable."

"You mean he might marry her?" the Earl asked in an incredulous tone.

"There is a possibility of it," the Dowager answered. "Zelée de Salône is not of noble birth, but on the other hand, she is not bourgeois."

"I have always thought César has said he has no intention of marrying again," the Earl remarked, "until he finds somebody with whom he is in love."

The Dowager made an expressive gesture with her hands.

"Love! What is love?" she asked. "And I am told on good authority that Zélee de Salône is determined to be his wife."

"And she, too, has been married before?"

"She was married for a short time to a man very much older than herself who died of a heart-attack. Since then I understand she has refused a number of suitors, but none of them, needless to say, were as important as César!"

"But surely," the Earl suggested, "he must realise it would be a mistake to marry anybody of whom the family disapproves?"

Lady Helmsdale sighed.

"As you well know, César has always been a law unto himself. His father married him off when he was only twenty to the daughter of the *Duc* de Vallon, which was in every way suitable both from the point of view of breeding and from the fact that the bride had a huge dowry."

The Earl did not speak, and the Dowager went on:

"You know what happened. The young couple loathed each other from the moment they had been united in Chartres Cathedral."

Her eyes were sad as she went on:

"After a year of what I have heard César describe as unutterable misery, the poor girl had a brain-storm which resulted in her becoming incurably insane and she died three years later."

"Knowing the circumstances, I have always been sorry for César," the Earl remarked.

"We all broke our hearts over him," the Dowager replied, "but there was nothing any of us could do. He travelled round the world and came back a changed man."

"What do you mean by that?" the Earl enquired.

"He had always been a little arrogant—what *Duc* has ever been anything else? But he had also become cynical and in a way much older than his years."

"At the same time, from all I have heard, he enjoyed himself!" the Earl remarked.

"He certainly caused a number of scandals in Paris, and fought several duels," Lady Helmsdale agreed. "At the same time, that is expected of a man who came into his title when still very young, and who finds himself, in the words of the poet, 'Monarch of all I survey'!"

The Earl laughed.

"That is certainly true where the *Ducs* de Montvéal are concerned! I have often thought that with that enormous Castle perched on top of a hill overlooking the vineyard-filled valley, no man could ask for a more impressive throne!"

The Dowager smiled.

"That is true, and ever since he has lived there, César has behaved like a King, or rather an Emperor, and what can we poor relations do but slavishly obey him?"

The Earl laughed again. Then he said:

"I have not seen César since his wife died, but of course I hear about him, and I cannot imagine that if he wishes to marry this woman of whom you disapprove, he will allow you or anyone else to interfere."

"That is why I do not intend to waste words," the Dowager said quietly, "but instead to produce—Yursa."

"And you are really thinking he will be interested in her?"

Lady Helmsdale gave a deep sigh.

"It is a gamble—of course it is a gamble! But it is the only way I can think of to divert him from suffering a matrimonial tragedy for the second time."

There was silence. Then the Earl said:

"I will not have Yursa forced to do anything she does not wish. I want above all things that she should be happy, as I was happy with your daughter."

"I know that, Edward," his mother-in-law said softly. "But Yursa is so lovely that I feel she would be wasted on any of the supercilious English aristocrats who, as you and I know, are interested only in hunting, shooting, and fishing, and paying little attention to their wives, however beautiful they may be."

The Earl threw back his head and laughed.

"You have always been very frank," he said, "and I must admit there is a grain of truth in what you say. However, is a Frenchman so very much more desirable, when his compliments are insincere, and while he kisses one woman's hand, his eyes are roving in search of another?"

"What I am hoping and praying, Edward," Lady Helmsdale said seriously, "is that César, who has never seen Yursa, will find her youth, her beauty, and her innocence are what he has been searching for in his heart."

"Do you think that possible?"

"No man who is brought up in Burgundy could be anything but romantic," the Dowager replied, "and I have loved César from the time he was born. There is Montvéal blood in my veins and his."

She paused before she continued:

"His mother, as you know, is my greatest and closest friend, and my own mother before her marriage was a Montvéal herself. I know that once he had ideals which may have been lost in the past years but I am sure are not entirely forgotten."

"You are an optimist," the Earl said. "A man who has been hurt and deeply disappointed will not any more than the leopard change his spots."

He was silent before he added slowly:

"If you ask me, César should marry a sophisticated, worldly woman who will understand him as no young and inexperienced girl is capable of doing."

"You may be right," Lady Helmsdale conceded, "but anything would be better than César marrying Zelée de Salône. In my opinion, although I have nothing to substantiate it, she is a wicked, basically evil woman, and if he marries her, he will regret it to his dying day!"

"That must be for him to decide," the Earl remarked, "and quite frankly, I have no wish for Yursa

7

to be mixed up with anything unpleasant, which might shock her."

There was a pause, then the Dowager said:

"All I am asking is that you will allow me to take Yursa to the *Château* on a visit. I am, as you know, always welcome whenever I wish to go there. I have only to ask César if I may bring somebody with me for him to acquiesce."

"You must promise me," the Earl replied, "that if I allow you to do this, you will not try to persuade Yursa to accept the *Duc* unless you are certain there is some chance of her finding happiness."

"You are insulting me," the Dowager protested. "I love César, but I also love my granddaughter. I would never harm Yursa in any way."

She looked blindly across the room before she said in a different tone:

"I have a feeling that she might be the salvation of a man who deserves better than to be tied to a woman who, as far as I am concerned, might be the spawn of the Devil himself!"

The Earl was startled.

"What makes you say that?" he asked.

The Dowager made an expressive gesture with her hand.

"I suppose, because my mother came from Burgundy, I have an acute perception. Anyway, my instinct tells me in a way I cannot express in words that I must take Yursa to the *Château*."

The Earl shrugged his shoulders.

"Since you put it in that way, I can only give my consent. At the same time, I trust you to do nothing which might endanger Yursa's happiness."

"On that I give you my sacred promise!" Lady Helmsdale said. "And now tell me how you are and what has been happening while I have been in France."

Yursa knew the conversation concerning her was at an end.

She had been standing listening at the door as if turned to stone, but now she went on tip-toe back the way she had come.

When she had almost reached the hall she turned and retraced her steps.

Running quickly down the passage, hoping her footsteps could be heard in the Study, she called out before she reached the door:

"Grandmama! I know that you are here!"

She burst into the room and ran towards her grandmother, who was sitting on the sofa.

The Dowager held out her arms.

"Yursa, my dear child!" she said. "How lovely to see you!"

"I have been wondering why you have not been to see us since you returned from France," Yursa said. "Did you have a lovely time in Paris and buy some enchanting new gowns?"

"I hope you will approve of them," her grandmother replied, "and I have brought quite a number for you, my dearest."

"Oh, Grandmama, how delightful! Papa has promised me some new ones to wear when we go to London, but I know nothing could be as smart as what is obtainable in Paris!"

"You should judge for yourself," the Dowager said.

She paused as she scrutinised her granddaughter,

thinking as she did so that she was even lovelier than she remembered.

It would, in fact, have been difficult for anyone who met her, unless he was blind, not to think that Yursa had stepped out of a fairy-story.

Her small oval face was dominated by two huge eyes which, instead of being blue to match her father's as might have been expected, were a strange mixture of grey with a touch of gold.

When, however, she was worried or unhappy, there was a purple tinge to them.

They were eyes that were certainly very different from those of other girls of her age.

Similarly, her translucent skin, which was as white as the petals of a magnolia, was enhanced by the strange, unusual lights in her hair.

It was gold—the deep gold of the hair in the pictures painted by Botticelli.

There was nothing insipid or dull about Yursa's hair; in fact, it seemed almost to sparkle and be part of the entrancing beauty of her smile.

It was a beauty, Lady Helmsdale thought, that could never be transmitted onto canvas because it was so vividly alive that there was nothing static about it.

Her whole being glowed with every movement she made, with every word she spoke, with every flutter of her eyelashes, which were darker than her hair.

She was beautiful, and it was an arresting beauty, a beauty that would hold and captivate a man so that he would find it hard to look away.

The Dowager put her hand over Yursa's.

"I have just been talking to your father, dearest child, and he has agreed that you should come with me to France for a few weeks before he takes you to London."

"Oh, Grandmama, how exciting!" Yursa exclaimed. "Will we be going to Paris?"

"Perhaps later, to buy you even more gowns. But first I want you to see the Castle that has always been very close to my heart since I was a young girl, and where your mother stayed when she was your age."

"You mean the *Château* de Montvéal?" Yursa exclaimed. "Oh, Grandmama, how wonderful! I would rather go there than anywhere else in the world!"

"That is what I hoped you would say," the Dowager said as she smiled, "and as I want to leave in three days' time, you must start packing at once."

Yursa clasped her hands together and looked at her father.

"I have agreed to this expedition," he said as if she had asked the question, "but if when you get there you are disappointed, your grandmother has promised to bring you home immediately."

"Why should I be disappointed?" Yursa enquired, but her father did not answer.

She knew later that night, when they sat talking together after dinner, that he was worried.

When they left the Dining-Room they went into the large Drawing-Room, where everything reminded the Earl of her mother.

"My dearest," he said to Yursa, "I want your happiness more than I want anything in the world!"

"I know that, Papa, and you have always been

11

very kind to me, and particularly since we lost Mama."

"I miss your mother more than I can say," the Earl admitted, "but I am fortunate that I have my daughter, and, of course, my two sons."

There was a glint in his eye as he spoke of John and William.

They were both with their Regiments, and he was excessively proud of them.

Yursa knew that while her father loved her, she took second place to her brothers.

It was this more than anything else which made her after her mother's death six years ago turn more and more to her fantasy world.

It was peopled with gods and goddesses, heroes and heroines, who were more real to Yursa than the persons with whom she came in contact every day.

At night she went to sleep telling herself stories of the men who had fought for their Faith and perhaps died for it.

And of the women who through prayer and the help of the Divine worked miracles.

Because her great-grandmother had been before her marriage a member of the Montvéal family, Yursa had always been proud of her French blood.

She had also, because her mother had been brought up a Catholic, been baptised into the Catholic faith, though her brothers were, like their father, Protestants.

It was an arrangement which had been adopted very successfully by a number of English noblemen who had married French women.

It made Yursa's life rather different from that of her English friends.

She not only worshipped in a different Church from the rest of her family, but she had been sent to be educated in a Convent in Normandy, part of which was a School for the children of aristocrats.

The Nuns, who were secluded and dedicated entirely to their faith, lived in another part of the Convent.

Although this appeared to make no difference to the happiness and love that existed between her father and mother, Yursa always felt there was a barrier between herself and the rest of the family.

In some ways she felt as if she were an outsider.

It was nothing she could put into words, and yet the feeling was there.

It therefore meant that she relied more and more on what she thought of as her own private world, which was always in her thoughts whatever she was doing.

Now, aware of what she had overheard at the door, she wondered if her father would express to her his anxiety about the visit she was to make with her grandmother.

Or perhaps he would just leave it unsaid.

She knew that there was a conflict going on inside him, and he was battling with himself, knowing it was his duty to prepare her in some way for what she might encounter when she reached France.

"Your grandmother," he said after a moment, "is very much looking forward to showing you the Castle which has meant so much to her all her life."

"She has often talked about it, Papa."

"It is certainly very magnificent," the Earl went on. "At the same time, you will find the Montvéals a somewhat strange family."

"What do you mean by that?"

"I mean," the Earl replied, "that they treat the *Duc*, who is still a comparatively young man, almost as if he were some omnipotent creature to whom they must bow down and obey, whatever he demands of them."

The Earl gave a short laugh before he went on:

"Our English Dukes are certainly well aware of their own consequence, but they do not seem to have the authority or to inspire the same feeling of awe that you will find at Montvéal."

Yursa did not reply, and after a moment her father went on:

"Do not let them intimidate you, my dear. After all, as my father always used to say, if you prick a King, he still bleeds like any other man!"

Yursa laughed.

"I will try not to be awe-struck, Papa. In any case, if he is as pompous as you say, I doubt if *Duc* César will even notice me."

"Just remember that if he does, he is just an ordinary man," the Earl said, "and in England, while we Love our heroes, we do not lie down and let them walk all over us!"

He spoke sharply and Yursa asked innocently:

"Is that what *Duc* César does?"

"I have not seen him for years," her father answered, "but from all I hear, he has become very stuck-up and needs taking down a peg or two—not that that is something you should attempt."

"No, of course not, Papa!"

"The trouble with all Frenchmen," the Earl went on, as if he were speaking to himself, "is that they think too much of themselves, not having been educated at a Public School, the same way as we are."

"Does that make a difference, Papa?"

"It certainly does! Your brothers will tell you that if they are 'cocky,' they soon have it kicked out of them, and a good job too!"

The Earl paused for a moment. Then he said:

"You are very young, Yursa, and I want you to realise there is no hurry for you to get married."

"No, of course not, Papa."

"I like having you here with me, and when we go to London, you will make a great many new friends of your own age. Of course, you can invite them back here when the Season is over."

"Thank you, Papa."

"What is more, they will be English, and when you do get married, I would like you to marry an Englishman—a decent chap who will love and respect you, and with whom you will be as happy as I was with your mother."

It was a long speech for the Earl to make. Yursa knew he was trying to find words with which to express his feelings, and it was not easy for him.

She got up from the chair in which she was sitting, and putting her arms around her father's neck as he stood with his back to the fireplace, she said:

"I love you, Papa, and I have no wish to do anything that would not please you."

The Earl put his arm around her.

"You are a good girl, Yursa. I do not pretend to

15

understand you at times, but I am very glad I have a daughter!"

"And I am very glad I have you as a father, Papa!" Yursa kissed his cheek.

Then as if he were embarrassed at having been over-emotional, the Earl began talking of their plans for the next morning and which horses they would be riding.

Only when she went up to bed did Yursa lie thinking of what she had overheard, feeling it strange that her grandmother should think it possible that she could change the *Duc*'s intention.

If he had really made up his mind to marry Zelée de Salône, it was unlikely in view of what her father had said about him that anyone could make him change it.

She had heard all sorts of things about César de Montvéal ever since she had been a small girl.

The fact that he was a *Duc* and a relative of her great-grandmother, and that her mother had always been a close friend of the family, made him seem like the Prince in a fairy-story.

His exploits and possessions were certainly different from anybody else's.

She had heard her mother talk of César until she felt she had met him, seen him, and listened to him.

Now, for the first time, all these things would become true.

She knew how excited she would have been at the mere idea of going to the *Château* with her grandmother if she had not overheard her conversation with her father.

But she now knew there was a very different reason for the visit, other than just to see the *Château*.

How was it possible that her grandmother could think for one instant that the *Duc* César would be interested in her, or that he would wish to marry a young, inexperienced girl from England?

At thirty-three he was a "man of the world" who apparently, from all she had overheard, had enjoyed many love-affairs.

Now he was comtemplating marrying a woman of whom his relatives disapproved.

Yursa was convinced that their opinion would not weigh in the slightest with the *Duc* unless he was very different from what she had been led to believe.

That he always expected to have his own way, that he organised his life entirely to his own satisfaction, had been impressed upon her since she had first heard of him.

She was quite certain now that if he wished to marry Zelée de Salône, he would do so regardless of anything anybody else might say about it.

She was well aware, and it had certainly been drilled into her, that aristocrats, both in France and England, married within their own class.

To make a *mésalliance* was to suffer endless indignity and unpleasantness, which was to be avoided at all costs.

She knew that her father and mother's marriage had been arranged.

Yet by a lucky chance they had, in fact, fallen deeply in love with each other even before they were engaged.

Their love had intensified year by year until,

when her mother died, her father had been broken-hearted.

Because he was a reserved man, the Earl had, as far as the outside world was concerned, concealed his misery and despair.

It was only because ever since she was a child Yursa had been very intuitive, that she had known how much her father suffered and how utterly miserable he was because his wife was no longer with him.

Because he was English, he could not express his feelings, even to her.

Yursa could communicate her sympathy and understanding only by being more extroverted in showing her feelings than she did naturally.

Now she knew what her father was feeling about her without his having to put it into words.

She was sure, although he did not say so, that he was shocked at the idea of her marrying the *Duc*, even though it would be a brilliant marriage from a social point of view.

She was sure he was thinking that the *Duc* would continue to create scandals, to pursue married women, and have *affaires de coeur*.

These were inevitably the talk not only of France, but also of England.

They were all matters which her father considered unpleasant and deeply deprecated, especially where they concerned a member of his own family.

She wanted to reassure him, to tell him she had no intention of marrying the *Duc* even if he asked her, which was unlikely.

She knew, however, that if she did so, she would have to reveal the fact that she had overheard the

18

conversation her father had had with her grandmother.

He would think it wrong and in a way "unsport-
ing" of her to have eavesdropped.

"Poor Papa!" Yursa said to herself in the darkness
of her room. "He is really worried about me, but
perhaps when we go to London I shall find some
charming and delightful Englishman of whom he will
approve."

It was wishful thinking.

At the same time, she could not help being
thrilled that she was to meet the redoubtable *Duc*
César for the first time.

She would then find out if he was as fascinating as
her grandmother thought he was. Also, if he was as
fast and improper as the shocked and lowered voices
of her other relatives who knew him indicated him to
be.

Yursa was, of course, very innocent.

At the Convent the conversation had covered
every subject except that of men.

That was a forbidden subject, and although occa-
sionally the other girls had giggled together over
what they had overheard during the School holidays,
Yursa had not been interested.

She was entranced by music, which seemed to be
a part of her dreams.

She had loved the literature she had been allowed
to read, and had found the History lessons fascinating
because through them she learnt more about France
than any other country in the world.

It was inevitable that she should be moved by the
piety of the Nuns, the mystic atmosphere she had

found in the Chapel, and the sincerity of the Priests who came to teach them about the Sacraments.

It was all part of the idealistic world in which she lived, and which absorbed her thoughts and her feelings to the exclusion of all else.

It was, too, in the beauty she found everywhere around her.

She was sure that just as she loved the flowers, the garden, the old oak trees in the Park, the streams running through the meadows, so she would love Burgundy.

She was also sure that she would love the huge *Château* standing sentinel over the valley and looking towards the far distant Jura mountains.

"Whatever the *Duc* is like," she told herself confidently, "I shall be thrilled with his environment, and the Kingdom over which he reigns."

Then she laughed at herself in the darkness, for just like all the other people who talked about him, she was thinking of him as a King, an Emperor.

A god to whom everybody must bow down!

That was something she had long ago determined she would not do, however difficult it might be to refuse.

chapter two

THE *Duc* de Montvéal stirred and yawned. Then as he moved the sheets, a soft, seductive voice beside him asked:

"You are not leaving me, *Mon Chèr?*"

"I think it is time I went back to my own room," the *Duc* replied.

"But, why? There is plenty of time."

The *Duc* yawned again, and it passed through his mind that he always found it boring when women wished to detain him after their love-making was over.

He was, in fact, tired, not only because he had been riding all day.

The hours he had spent with Zelée had been fiery, tempestuous, and although he did not like to admit it, extremely exhausting.

Then, as she put her head on his shoulder, he heard her say:

"I want to talk to you, César."

"I should have thought that this was hardly the time for conversation," he replied with a slightly sarcastic note in his voice.

"It is easier than when we are consumed with the fires of love."

The *Duc* wondered vaguely if he should put her to one side and rise as he wished to do, or whether he would be wiser to listen to what she had to say.

He could not be sure what it could be, but he knew Zelée's methods all too well.

He was certain she was going to demand of him something very expensive which he would find it hard to refuse when he was not thinking as clearly as he did usually.

He felt her draw even closer to him, and he asked with a touch of irritation in his voice:

"Well, what is it?"

"I have been thinking, my most beloved and perfect lover, that we should be married!"

For a moment the *Duc* was lost for words.

He had never at any time contemplated marrying Zelée, and it had never entered his mind that it was something she might want.

She had made no secret of the fact that there had been many lovers in her life since the death of her husband, and more than likely before it also.

The *Duc* had taken her as his mistress as he had taken a great number of other women, without thought of there being any permanency about it.

Zelée admittedly was slightly different from the

demi-mondaines with whom he enjoyed himself in Paris.

She came from a respectable French family.

She had been married to a man who was not noble, but was certainly respected in the part of France where they lived, not far from the *Château*.

Her behaviour, however, had made the more straight-laced Dowagers ostracise her.

The *Duc* looked on her as having the same standing as the actresses who amused him, and the Courtesans of Paris, who had become notorious all over Europe.

He knew she was waiting for an answer, and after a moment he replied lightly:

"My dear Zelée, I should make an abominable husband if I married, and actually it is a position I have so far managed to avoid."

"I have heard that before," Zelée replied, "but, *Mon Brave*, we would be very happy together, and I will keep you amused where with any other woman you would be bored within a few months."

This the *Duc* had to admit was true.

He had always thought that whoever he married, it was a situation that would pall once the honeymoon was over.

But that also included Zelée!

Although he found her amusing and more passionate than any woman he had ever encountered before, it was not something he would think admirable in the woman he married.

If he thought he had answered Zelée's question effectively, he was mistaken.

"You must be aware, my dearest," she said in a

coaxing tone which he sometimes found irresistible, "that my father and my other relatives are perturbed that I should be staying here for so long, and they expect you to protect my reputation."

The *Duc* almost laughed aloud.

He knew only too well that Zelée's reputation in the neighbourhood was a disgrace to her family.

She had also, admittedly through her association with him, become notorious in Paris.

That she was beautiful went without saying, but she had a strange, rather savage beauty that was different from that of most other women.

The darkness of her hair, the way her eyes slanted a little upwards at the corners, the twisting smile that was undeniably provocative, made artists beg on their knees to be allowed to paint her.

Journalists wrote about her on every possible occasion, their adjectives overflowing in their efforts to describe her adequately.

She was, in fact, the *Duc* thought, almost indescribable.

There was something primitive and peculiarly French about her, which was in a way slightly inhuman.

Her sharp wit, her very twisted sense of humour, amused him.

Yet he could understand all too well why every member of his family disliked her, and resented her being so often a guest at the *Château*.

It would have made it outrageous to have her stay there alone.

There were always house-parties, therefore, where married women, whether they liked it or not, played chaperone to the *Duc* and the woman they could not dismiss by saying she came from the gutter.

A number of them knew Zelée's father and uncles, who were all well off and owned properties in Burgundy or on the borders of it.

"We will be very happy," Zelée was whispering, "and, of course, I will provide you with the son you must have to inherit."

It was then the *Duc* had a feeling of revulsion.

He was not shocked by anything he had done—why should he be?

At the same time, it was impossible to think of Zelée as the mother of his son—indeed, of anybody's children.

With a stiff movement that was characteristic of him he set her on one side and rose from the bed, saying as he did so:

"You are talking nonsense! As you well know, I am determined to marry no one, but to enjoy my freedom."

As he spoke he shrugged himself into the long robe he had left lying on a chair.

Only as he tied the sash around his slim waist above his narrow hips did he realise that Zelée had not replied.

She was looking at him with her strange dark, slanting eyes in a manner he did not understand.

Then as he bent to take her hand and kiss it with a courtesy that was part of his upbringing, she said very softly:

"You are mine, César, and I will never give you up!"

His lips barely touched her skin before he turned from the bed to walk across the room and quietly open the door.

He did not look back, although she was waiting for him to do so.

Only when the door had closed behind him and she realised he had gone did she make a sound that was like a rumbling roar in a tiger's throat.

'You are mine! Mine!' she wanted to scream at him.

Then she flung herself back against the pillows and told herself she would hold him however hard he might try to escape.

* * *

It was at breakfast the next morning that the *Duc* remembered to say to his cousin, an attractive *Marquise*, that a relative, Lady Helmsdale, was arriving to stay.

"Oh, I am glad!" she exclaimed. "I have not seen her for some time and she is one of the most charming old ladies I have ever met! I hope when I get to her age I am exactly like her."

The *Duc* smiled.

"That is a long way ahead, but I agree with you. Elizabeth Helmsdale has a charm that is ageless, and I am always delighted to see her."

"We must ask some of her old *beaux* to dinner," the *Marquise* suggested.

"Of course, but we must also ask some young *beaux* as well," the *Duc* replied.

The *Marquise* raised her very elegantly pencilled eye-brows, and he explained:

"The Countess is bringing her granddaughter, Yursa Holme, to stay."

"How old is she?"

The *Duc* thought for a moment.

"I have heard my mother speak of her, and I think she must be seventeen or eighteen."

"Good heavens!" the *Marquise* exclaimed. "She will find us a very old party! Where am I to find some charming young men of twenty or twenty-one?"

"I am sure they are there if you look for them," the *Duc* replied indifferently.

The *Marquise* was silent for a moment, then she said:

"I think, César, it would be wise, if we are to have a débutante in our midst, that *Madame* de Salône should terminate what has already been a very long visit."

She knew she was being outrageous in speaking so openly.

For a moment she thought the *Duc* would be angry at her, and she wondered nervously if she had gone too far.

To her surprise, however, he replied:

"Perhaps you are right, and it would be a good idea if you concentrate on having young people to stay, which will give us an excuse to dispense with some of my other guests."

As he finished speaking he rose from the table and left the Dining-Room, and the *Marquise* stared after him in amazement.

Then as she felt as if she could breathe again, she wondered if *Madame* de Salône's hold over the *Duc* was waning.

When he was not present, the family talked of little else, and the *Marquise* knew they were terrified that she might in some magical way change his determination to remain a bachelor.

"I hate her!" the *Marquise* said to herself.

She was expressing what every other woman in the *Château* felt about Zelée de Salône.

She had, they thought, although they could not prove it, an evil influence on their beloved César.

To everybody's astonishment, Zelée informed them that afternoon that she was leaving on the following day.

For a moment following her announcement there was complete silence.

Then as if those listening were embarrassed by their thoughts, they all began talking at once.

* * *

Travelling through France with her grandmother was the most exciting thing Yursa had ever known.

She had been thrilled from the moment they crossed the Channel into the land to which she always felt she belonged.

This was not because she had been at School there, but because she was proud that a little of her blood was French.

It was a long and tiring journey to reach the *Château*, but it was as if it all passed in the flash of a second as she stared out of the windows of the train.

She had always longed to see more of France than Normandy, which was very like England.

Now she looked from the carriage at the great vistas of rich cultivated land, at the distant mountains silhouetted against the sky, and at the long straight roads bordered by trees.

When at last she saw the *Château* standing high on a steep hill overlooking the valley, it was exactly how she had imagined it.

Its towers and turrets made it seem enormous, and jutting out at one side was the steeple of the private Chapel in which she knew the *Duc*s of Montvéal were buried.

As if she wanted Yursa to capture the atmosphere of her beloved France, her grandmother talked to her all the way of the history of the family and of Burgundy itself.

She said very little about the *Duc*, and yet Yursa knew perceptively that he was always in her mind.

She could read her grandmother's thoughts and knew that more than anything else she wanted her granddaughter to be the *Duchesse* de Montvéal.

The *Duc*'s superb horses, which had been waiting for them with an elegant, well-sprung carriage at the station, pulled them slowly up a drive of huge trees which met overhead.

It seemed as if the *Château* touched the sky itself, and Yursa was caught up in a spell of enchantment.

How could she be anything else when everything was so beautiful?

The secret dreams that had held her captive since she was very small had at last materialised into reality.

The entrance to the *Château* was impressive: huge oak doors opened into the court-yard and a flight of stone steps led to the front-door.

On each side stood carved in stone the heraldic

animals that featured in the Montvéal coat of arms.

Because they had been travelling all day, Lady Helmsdale insisted that they go straight to their bedrooms.

"We must rest," she told the Major Domo, "and change before we meet our host.

"There is sure to be a large party," she told Yursa, "for, as you know, French houses, unlike those in England, make every member of the family welcome whenever they wish to come."

"What happens if they all arrive together, and there is no room for them all?" Yursa asked.

Her grandmother laughed.

"There are more rooms in the *Château* than I have ever been able to count, and I am quite sure nobody would ever be sent away, however crowded it might seem."

Yursa had learned that the *Duc* enjoyed having people round him, and was extremely hospitable.

It was something he had inherited from his father and his grandfather, and many generations before them.

This in turn was something they had inherited from the ancient *Ducs* of Burgundy who, if history was to be believed, entertained royally all their lives.

She knew Yursa was listening intently as she said:

"Philip the Good was the greatest Valois *Duc*. He loved chivalry, founded the Order of the Golden Fleece and his own Order of Chivalry. He received at his Ducal Court Ambassadors of all the Kings and Emperors of the time."

"And is that what the *Duc* César does now?" Yursa asked.

"Anyone who is invited to the *Château* feels it is an honour," the Dowager replied. "At the same time, César is a young man and he does not entertain those only who are successful but also those who decorate the *Château* like flowers."

Yursa knew that her grandmother was speaking of women.

For the first time she wondered if she would look dull and perhaps dowdy amongst the French women who were not only beautiful, but invariably *chic*.

Then she remembered the delightful gowns that her grandmother had brought for her from Paris, and thought that as far as clothes were concerned, she should be able to hold her own.

It was very unusual for her to think about herself, and when they entered the *Château*, there was so much to see, so much to absorb.

She was walking down the stairs beside her grandmother after they had rested, bathed, and changed for dinner, when she remembered the conversation she had overheard outside her father's Study.

In fact, she had forgotten in her excitement at reaching the *Château* that the reason for the visit was that her grandmother and apparently the *Duc's* mother thought she might make a suitable bride for him.

"I am sure there is no chance of such a thing happening," Yursa reassured herself.

Yet she was still excited at the thought of meeting him.

There were footmen dressed in elaborate livery, powdered wigs, and white silk stockings, to direct them towards the Reception Room.

As two of them flung open the doors the Major Domo, even more resplendent than the others, announced their names, and Yursa felt she was entering Fairyland.

It was not surprising, for already the huge chandeliers had been lit.

The whole room seemed to shimmer with light, so that it was for the moment difficult to see anything but a kaleidoscope of colour and beauty.

Then through what seemed a haze there came a man so startlingly different from what she had expected that Yursa gave a little gasp.

He was taller than most Frenchmen and had an athletic figure which might have made him a warrior like the original *Ducs*.

His hair was very dark and brushed back from a square forehead, and his features were almost classical but had an originality about them which made him different from any other man.

This was perhaps because his dark eyes, bold and penetrating, seemed to take in everything, seeing not only what was on the surface but what lay within the person at whom he was looking.

Then because of the twist to his lips and the lines which ran from his nose to his mouth, she thought there was something cynical and at the same time raffish about him.

It made him, Yursa thought, look like a pirate or a buccaneer, and certainly not what she would have expected of a *Duc*.

Yet at the same time he looked omnipotent and overwhelmingly authoritative.

It made her, despite herself, curtsy a little lower

than she had intended, and she found it difficult to meet his eyes.

First he bent and kissed Lady Helmsdale's hand, then her cheek, saying as he did so:

"It is enchanting to see you again! I cannot tell you how glad I am that you are here!"

"It is what I have been looking forward to for a long time," the Dowager replied, "and you are so kind to let me bring my granddaughter with me."

She indicated Yursa with her hand, and as she curtsied the *Duc* said:

"I am delighted to welcome you, Lady Yursa. But must we, seeing that we are distantly related, be formal? I shall call you Yursa, which is how I have always heard of you."

"I am honoured, *Monsieur*," Yursa managed to say.

She knew as his eyes flickered over her that he was surprised at her appearance.

She wondered if it was because she was smarter than he might have expected of an English débutante.

She had no idea that the *Duc* was, in fact, astonished by her beauty.

Lady Helmsdale and Yursa were then introduced to the other guests of whom there seemed to be, as they had expected, a large number.

Many of them were, Yursa learnt, relatives of the *Duc*, and therefore distant connections of her own.

While they were sorting out the very complex family tree, the last guest made an appearance.

While the women thought scornfully that it was so like Zelée to make a dramatic entrance in order to make out she was more important than she really was, the *Duc* was amused.

He was well aware that Zelée never did anything conventional and never missed an opportunity of drawing attention to herself.

To-night she had succeeded in being immediately the focus of everybody's attention.

She was wearing a Worth gown, but it was not the typical elegance of his creation which commanded attention, but the colour he had used.

All in flaming red Frederick Worth had combined satin, lace, sequins, and tulle with his usual genius. The startling effect was accentuated by the darkness of Zelée's hair with its blue lights, and the whiteness of her skin.

She looked as if she had stepped straight out of the flames of a blazing fire.

Or, as one or two of the women thought spitefully, out of Hell itself.

Round her neck she wore a collar of rubies and diamonds, and the same stones glittered in her ears and on her wrists.

To Yursa, who had thought the other ladies in the party were strikingly elegant, Zelée was a revelation.

She had never imagined that any woman could look so fantastic and yet at the same time so beautiful.

She advanced slowly, very slowly, down the room, and when the *Duc* moved to meet her, she put out her hand and quite outrageously touched his cheek.

It was a gesture of love and it was also as if she were proclaiming to the world her possession of him.

It was then that Yursa realised who she was and

knew this was the woman of whom her grandmother had been talking to her father.

'She is so beautiful,' she thought to herself, 'and of course he is in love with her.'

Then as the *Duc* drew Zelée across the room to meet her grandmother, Yursa had a different impression.

Lady Helmsdale greeted her very coldly though politely, but there was a note in her voice which told Yursa only too well that she disapproved.

Then she heard the *Duc* say:

"Let me introduce you to Lady Yursa Holme, who is a distant cousin of mine."

Zelée turned towards her with a grace and a smile.

But as she looked at Yursa, the smile vanished and her dark eyes which had seemed to shine in the light of the chandeliers became suddenly hard.

It was as if she recognised Yursa as a rival.

She seemed suddenly to become tense and to vibrate with an enmity that was unmistakable.

Then strangely, because she had not expected it, Yursa felt the same.

Now she realised in the passing of a second why her grandmother had said that Zelée was the spawn of Satan, and she knew that she was evil.

Her feelings were so intense that they startled her.

As Zelée turned away with a flounce, slipping her arm through the *Duc*'s, she knew that she had for the first time in her life encountered an enemy.

Without being aware of how it had happened, she was at war.

* * *

They proceeded into dinner, the *Duc* escorting the Dowager, as she was the latest arrival.

The *Marquise* sat at one end of the table as his hostess, and Zelée to her intense annoyance was not, as she had expected, on the *Duc's* left.

It was the position she had occupied ever since she had arrived at the *Château* and she knew this was why earlier in the afternoon César had insisted that she should go home to-morrow.

"Why?" she had asked him. "What is the hurry? I am so happy to be with you."

"I know," he replied, "but my mother's closest friend, Lady Helmsdale, is arriving and, although her mother was my relative, she is very English in her ways, and I must certainly be circumspect while she is staying with me."

"So you are turning me out!" Zelée said defiantly.

"I am asking you to leave while she is here."

Zelée had shrugged her shoulders very expressively.

"Why should you trouble yourself with the English, who are dull, frumpish, and usually very plain?"

"I am not considering them so much as my mother," the *Duc* replied, "for I know she would feel humiliated if she thought I was behaving badly while Lady Helmsdale was at the *Château*. Tales of my behaviour would be told and re-told in England."

"Is it behaving badly to love you and for us to find an inexpressible bliss when we are together?" Zelée asked softly.

36

"I am asking you to be sensible," the *Duc* said patiently.

"That is something I have never been able to be for long," Zelée replied.

Then, as if she knew he was determined, she was too clever to make a scene.

"Very well, César," she said, "I will go home for a week, or however long it is that your boring English friends are here, but you will find it very dull without me, and the nights will seem empty and long."

She spoke the words in a voice almost as if she were hypnotising him into believing what she wanted him to believe.

But he merely replied:

"Thank you, and tell Hélène that you are leaving. It will come better from you than from me."

Hélène was the *Marquise*, whom Zelée disliked, and she shrugged her shoulders.

At the same time, he was aware that she was sensible enough to know that what he was saying was right.

She had, however, because Zelée was Zelée, to make quite a scene about it when most of the party were gathered in the Salon later in the afternoon.

When the *Duc* came into the room, Zelée had run towards him to say:

"*Mon Chèr!* I am desolated, but alas, it is unavoidable!"

"What is?" the *Duc* enquired.

"That I must leave you. I have had a message from my father to say that my little dog whom I love very dearly has had an accident. There is no one to comfort him as well as I can, so I must go home."

The *Duc*'s eyes were twinkling as Zelée elaborated on her misery at leaving, and also her distress at such an unfortunate occurrence when she was away from home.

Only when they were alone for a few seconds before everyone had gone upstairs to change did Zelée ask:

"You are pleased with me—yes? That I am leaving as you ordered me to do."

"It was slightly over-dramatic," the *Duc* replied mockingly. "But thank you for doing what I wanted."

"I only hope you will miss me and that every moment I am not with you you will find it so boring that you will be crying out for me to return!"

She moved a little nearer to him as she spoke, and although she was not touching him, he felt as though she encircled him with her desires.

"To-night," she whispered, "I will leave you waiting for me with a hunger that cannot be assuaged until we are together again."

She looked up into his eyes as she spoke, then moved away with the sensuousness of a snake, gliding silently over the carpet.

The *Duc* watched her go until she finally disappeared.

Then he gave himself a little shake, as if to free himself of the mesmeric bonds with which she had tied him.

Yursa thought dinner was like watching an exquisite picture come to life.

She was aware, although she tried not to think about it, of the hostile glances she received from Zelée, who was sitting on the other side of the table.

Once again she could feel a hatred that was unmistakable.

She tried not to think about it, but it was impossible not to be aware that this strange and beautiful woman loathed her.

She wondered if perhaps she, too, had overheard what the *Duc*'s mother and her grandmother had been planning.

Then she told herself, now that she had seen the *Duc* with his friends, and, of course, Zelée, that the whole thing was preposterous.

Only two old women with nothing better to do could think of anything so unlikely.

The *Duc* never glanced in her direction, and she thought that he was completely oblivious of anyone of so little importance.

Also she was convinced it would never strike him that his mother would plan to link his future with an unknown young woman from England.

"He is French, they are all French, and I am quite certain that his mother would resent it and find it intolerable for the *Duc* to marry anyone but a completely French wife," she told herself.

She could understand that they were afraid of Zelée, but that was something different.

She was, Yursa thought, like the fire she embodied so vividly in her gown, a fire which could easily burn those she disliked.

Yursa felt herself give a little shiver.

Then common sense told her to ignore anything that might spoil the magic she felt at being at the *Château* and seeing so many treasures.

After dinner, when they all moved to the Salon,

the men accompanying the women as was usual in France and not staying behind to drink port, Yursa went to the window.

The night was dark and the stars were shining overhead.

The valley below seemed far away and very mysterious.

She found herself thinking of the battles that must have been fought there in the past, and how Philip the Good, despite his name, had helped the English during the last stages of the Hundred Years' War.

One of his soldiers had dragged Joan of Arc from her saddle under the walls of Compiègne and sold her to the English for ten-thousand crowns, well aware of what her fate would be.

She was so deep in her thoughts that Yursa started when a deep voice beside her said:

"You find it beautiful?"

She turned to find that *Duc* César was beside her, but she had not heard him approach.

"It is even lovelier than I expected," she said.

"I suspect that your grandmother has talked to you of the *Château*."

"And ever since, it has been in my dreams," Yursa answered.

"And you are not disappointed now that you have seen it?"

"It is everything I expected . . . and more! How very, very lucky you are to own it and be the *Duc!*"

He looked at her in surprise, and there was a faintly cynical look in his eyes as he said:

"Am I also what you expected?"

"No . . . you are quite . . . different!"

It was not the answer he usually received, and the *Duc* asked curiously:

"In what way am I different?"

Yursa thought for a moment, not looking at him, but staring out into the darkness.

"I am waiting," he said after a moment, "because I am interested."

"I was thinking what the difference is," Yursa answered. "I think it is because you are . . . more alive and very much more . . . intuitive than I had expected . . . you to be."

"How do you know I am intuitive?"

She made a little gesture which expressed better than words that it was something she felt but for which there was no easy explanation.

"What else do you think about me now that we have met?" he asked.

He knew, as he spoke, he had nearly added: 'Instead of just being in your dreams,' and somehow he did not think it conceited that he should expect to be there.

It was really inevitable, as if he knew that it would be impossible for her grandmother to speak about the *Château* without including him.

"I was told," Yursa said after a moment, "that they think of you as a King, an Emperor, even perhaps a god!"

"Is that what you feel I am?"

She shook her head.

"Then—what am I?" the *Duc* asked.

Yursa turned her head away from the valley and the stars.

"You are the *Duc* de Montvéal," she replied, "and that should be enough for any man!"

The *Duc* was surprised.

He was used to flattery, to women extolling his appearance, his talents, and his intelligence.

Now he knew that he was probing into Yursa's mind, but she had circumvented him in what was a clever way, telling him nothing and yet giving him an answer that was irrefutable.

He wanted to go on talking to her, but at that moment Zelée was beside him and her arm went through his.

"I am waiting for you to come and play cards with me," she said, pouting, "and you cannot refuse me on our last evening."

She drew him away.

Yursa went on looking out of the window until one of her elderly relations joined her to talk about the family links and how many generations there were between them.

*   *   *

It was late when everybody went up to bed.

There was a maid servant waiting in Yursa's bedroom to help her undress.

When she put on the pretty nightgown and attractive negligée which her grandmother had bought for her in Paris, she walked again to the window to look out over the darkened countryside.

She could see a light here and there and it was to her as if a star had fallen from the sky.

Once again she was thinking of the past, of the

soldiers, the battles, and the *Ducs* who had fought here and perhaps lost their lives.

Then unexpectedly the door of her bed-room opened and she turned in surprise to see Zelée de Salône standing there.

Yursa moved from the window, letting the curtain fall behind her, wondering what this beautiful woman could want with her at this hour of the night.

Zelée shut the door behind her and said:

"Before I leave to-morrow, as I have to do, there is something I wish to say to you, Lady Yursa."

There was an ominous note in her voice which told Yursa before she spoke that she intended to be disagreeable.

"I cannot imagine what you have to say," Yursa replied, "but perhaps you would like to sit down?"

She indicated an armchair as she spoke, but Zelée still stood by the door.

In her flamboyant gown she seemed almost to burn up the beauty of the bed-room, with its painted ceiling and soft damask hangings.

"What I have to say," she began, "is very simple— the *Duc* is mine, and nothing you can say or do can take him away from me!"

She seemed almost to spit the words, and Yursa stiffened and took a step backwards almost as if Zelée had assaulted her.

"I knew as soon as I saw you," Zelée went on, "why you have been brought here by that old harridan, your grandmother, who has been scheming with the *Duchesse* to marry you to César for the past five years. Well, you will fail, do you hear me? You will fail!"

She spoke intensely, still with that fire that Yursa felt was almost physical.

"I am warning you!" Zelée continued. "If you try to interfere between us, it will be something you will regret! Go back to England and leave the *Duc* alone!"

Her last words seemed to echo round the room.

Then, as Zelée turned swiftly to open the door, she looked back.

"Go away," she warned, "before it is too late!"

As Yursa stood silent, finding it impossible to speak, Zelée went from the room, and the door closed behind her.

For a moment Yursa just stood transfixed.

It was not only what Zelée had said, it was once again the strange vibrations and violent hatred coming from her that rendered Yursa speechless and immobile.

Then, as she walked to a chair and sat down, she realised she was trembling.

Although it seemed absurd, she was more afraid of the woman who had just confronted her than anything she had ever encountered before in her whole life.

chapter three

YURSA did not sleep well and had a restless night.

She found herself haunted by the Frenchwoman's flashing eyes and the harsh note in her voice.

She told herself over and over again that it was childish to be frightened of any woman, especially one who was leaving Montvéaĺ.

Yet she felt a little shiver go through her, and only after she had prayed for a long while to her mother and the Saints did she fall asleep.

When she woke she knew the one thing she did not want was to see *Madame* de Salône before she left the *Château*.

Therefore, when her maid Jeanne called her she asked tentatively:

"Have you any idea what time *Madame* de Salône is leaving?"

The maid shot her a sharp glance as if she thought

she had a reason for asking before she replied:

"*Madame* is leaving after *petit déjeuner, M'mselle*, but she is taking it in her bed-room."

Yursa gave a little sigh of relief.

Then as Jeanne turned away she saw the maid surreptitiously cross herself, and thought it was a strange thing to do.

She was, however, so determined not to risk an unfortunate encounter that when she was dressed she went down a side staircase which she had learned the previous evening would take her near to the stables.

She supposed it was quite usual in the *Château*, as it was in her father's house, that guests, if they felt in need of fresh air before breakfast, would visit the stables.

She expected the *Duc*'s stables to be magnificent.

Yet when she saw them she was impressed to find them even better built and certainly more commodious than she had expected.

Never had she seen better bred or finer horses, and the Head Groom took her from stall to stall, gratified by her exclamations of delight at every animal they inspected.

They had just finished one row of stalls and were about to start another, when the Groom turned away from her and Yursa saw the *Duc* coming into the stable.

He was looking extremely smart in his riding-clothes, and when he saw her he exclaimed:

"So this is where you are! Cousin Hélène was wondering at breakfast what had happened to you."

"I am sorry if I have been . . . rude," Yursa said quickly, "but I came just to have a quick look at your horses and have been so entranced by them that I stayed much . . . longer than I . . . intended."

"*M'mselle* has a way with horses, Your Grace!" the Head Groom said.

"In that case," the *Duc* replied, "I expect you would like to ride."

Yursa's eyes lit up.

"I was hoping you would . . . allow me to . . . do so."

The *Duc* looked at his watch.

"I came here to decide which of my horses I would ride this morning," he said, "and if you can change and have something to eat in fifteen minutes, you can accompany me."

Yursa gave a cry of delight that sounded like the song of a small bird.

Without even replying, she picked up the front of her gown and ran from the stable into the yard as quickly as she could and back into the *Château*.

Jeanne was still in her bed-room and she helped Yursa to change quickly into her riding-habit.

It was not very smart, nor new, but since she had grown a little since it was made for her, it revealed the smallness of her waist and the curve of her breasts.

Because, too, it was of a dark material, which was considered correct in an English hunting-field, it threw into prominence the translucence of her skin and the vivid gold of her hair.

She had changed in ten minutes and ran down the stairs into the Dining-Room, where several members of the house-party were still eating breakfast.

They paid little attention to her as she quickly ate a hot croissant with butter and honey, and drank a cup of coffee.

47

Only as she slipped hastily out of the room did one of the older ladies say to the *Marquise:*

"That is a very attractive girl and certainly gives herself no airs and graces!"

"Why should she?" the *Marquise* asked with a smile.

The older woman shrugged her shoulders.

"I find the young women to-day, especially the pretty ones, are very spoilt. They think of nothing but themselves."

The *Marquise* laughed.

"I remember the same criticism being made about my generation and the generation before me!"

Unaware that she was being complimented, Yursa ran as fast as she could to the stables to find the *Duc* already mounted on a magnificent black stallion.

The grooms were holding a horse almost the equal of his for her.

Yursa had ridden since she could walk, so she was not afraid that she would disgrace herself in front of the *Duc*.

Indeed, she was so delighted at having such a fine mount that she almost forgot he was accompanying her.

They rode out of the stable-yard, down the drive, and Yursa realised they were going towards some level ground in the valley.

They had almost passed through the thick woods which covered the hill on which the *Château* stood, when there was the sound of wheels behind them.

Automatically Yursa and the *Duc* drew their horses onto the grass verge to be out of the way.

Then as Yursa looked towards the approaching car-

riage she saw a face at the window and realised it was
Madame de Salône.

For a moment the dark, slanting eyes were on her,
and once again she could feel the vibration of hate.

As the *Duc* swept off his hat politely, the carriage
passed them, and there was only the rumble of the
wheels dying away into the distance.

For a moment Yursa felt as if she could not move
and was frozen to the spot.

Then, as her horse swished his tail and fidgeted to
be off, she forced herself to move forward in the direction in which they had been going before they
heard the carriage behind them.

She must, however, have looked very pale, and
her eyes frightened, or perhaps he was just using his
instinct, for the *Duc* said:

"Why does *Madame* de Salône upset you?"

There was a tremor in Yursa's voice as she replied:

"She . . . she frightens . . . me!"

"Why should she do that?"

Too late Yursa wished she had said nothing, and
she turned her face away from the *Duc* hoping he
would think she had not heard his question.

He knew, however, there was something wrong,
and drawing his horse nearer to hers, he said:

"Tell me! I want to know how she has frightened
you."

She wanted to refuse to answer, but found it impossible.

"She . . . she came to my . . . room last . . . night."

"To your room? What for?"

"She was . . . angry and . . . upset."

The *Duc*'s lips tightened.

49

He was too intelligent not to realise that Zelée had made a scene and there was no need to ask why.

After a moment he said almost sharply:

"Forget her! She is of no importance to you."

"No...and it is...foolish of me to be... frightened."

Yursa spoke like a child who was trying to be brave in the dark, and the *Duc* smiled before he asked:

"Are you often frightened?"

"I cannot remember...ever being...frightened of a person...before," Yursa replied because he was obviously expecting an answer.

The *Duc* frowned, then, as if he thought it was better to talk of what had happened rather than ignore it, he said:

"*Madame* de Salône is very unpredictable, and has, as you must have noticed, a penchant for the theatrical and the over-dramatic. So as I have already said, forget her!"

"I...I will.. try," Yursa said meekly.

Then she thought she was being like the rest of the family, obeying orders without questioning them just because he gave them.

With a smile that swept away the fear in her eyes and brought the colour back into her cheeks, she said:

"Now you are behaving like the Emperor or god whom we spoke of last night. You must be aware that you can direct people's actions, but...not their... thoughts."

The *Duc* laughed.

"That is certainly an original idea which has not occurred to me before."

"It is true," Yursa said. "I have often found that the more you try to forget something... the more tenaciously it... remains in your... mind."

When he considered it, the *Duc* knew this was true.

He had the uncomfortable feeling that while he was trying to forget Zelée's demand that he should marry her, her proposal kept recurring in his thoughts.

By this time they had reached the valley.

There was a level field of grass ahead of them, and the *Duc* said:

"Before we become too serious, let us please our horses by racing them to where in the distance you will see a white post."

That was something Yursa longed to do. She flashed him a glance of delight and they were off.

She knew she had no chance, however skillfully she rode, of beating the *Duc* on his magnificent stallion, but at least she managed to keep up with him.

They passed the white post, which she learnt later was just over a mile from where they had started, riding neck and neck.

When they drew in their horses a little farther on, the *Duc* said:

"You ride magnificently, as I expect a great number of people have already told you."

"My father has always been very particular that I should have a good seat and soft hands."

"You ride like Diana, the Goddess of the Chase."

Although she was pleased at the compliment, Yursa suspected it was something the *Duc* had said many times before to a large number of other women.

They rode on more slowly.

Now the *Duc* was showing her the vineyards, and she thought the long rows of beautifully kept vines were exceedingly attractive.

Finding she was interested, the *Duc* told her of the great red wines of Burgundy: Gevrey-Chambertin, Nuit-St-Georges, Clos Vougeot, and Romanée-Conti, soon to be decimated by the dreaded Phylloxeria.

"My favourite," he said, "if you are interested, is the Gevrey-Chambertin. You may have heard that Napoléon Bonaparte enjoyed and drank a half-bottle of it at every meal."

"How interesting!" Yursa exclaimed.

"One of the many burdens he had to bear while he was on St. Helena," the *Duc* went on, "was that he was not provided with it and had to drink ordinary claret. He missed his Gevrey-Chambertin."

It was the sort of story that Yursa found interesting, and the *Duc* told her many tales of the district as they rode homewards.

"They are very primitive here," he said. "The villagers still believe there are Dragons in the forests and nymphs in the streams."

He laughed before he added:

"Besides, of course, Witches, who tell fortunes and concoct love-potions for the girls to entice the men they desire."

"Do their spells ever work?" Yursa enquired.

"The peasants say they do, and that, of course, is three-quarters of the battle."

"When I was small," Yursa told him, "there was supposed to be a Witch in our village, but she died before I was old enough to visit her."

"Why should you be interested in Witches?" the *Duc* enquired.

There was a little pause before Yursa replied:

"I suppose I have always been ... interested in anything that was ... mysterious, or perhaps the right word is ... 'Supernatural.'"

"Why?"

She thought for a moment before she answered:

"I have always believed it is due to my French blood that I sometimes have an instinct about people which comes from a ... power that is ... outside myself."

As she spoke, she made a little gesture with her hands and said:

"I am explaining it very badly. Perhaps it could be expressed better by the word 'Intuition.'"

"What you are really saying," the *Duc* said, "is that you hear voices, like Joan of Arc."

"Perhaps that is the ... explanation," Yursa agreed, "but all I know is that I am aware when ... something unusual will ... happen before it does ... and I am never ... mistaken."

"Then you definitely have the voices in which we all believe, and they are a gift to those who have the blood of Burgundy in their veins."

"That is a lovely thing to say to me!" Yursa replied.

She looked so happy with her eyes shining in the sunlight, which also seemed to shimmer on her hair.

The *Duc* thought she could not have been more

delighted if he had given her a diamond bracelet or a ruby necklace.

Then he shied away from the thought of Zelée and told himself his horses were carrying her a long way from the *Château*.

She would not dare to come back until he permitted her to, and perhaps that would be never.

When they returned to the house, Yursa's grandmother was waiting in the hall.

"I was told you had gone riding, my child," she said to Yursa. "You have enjoyed yourself?"

"It was wonderful!" Yursa replied. "I have never ridden such a magnificent horse before!"

She saw her grandmother, as she spoke, glance at the *Duc*, and knew that she very nearly added: "Or with such a magnificent escort!"

Because that made her ride seem contrived instead of something which had occurred just by chance, Yursa hurried up the stairs to change without even looking at the *Duc*.

When she came down, it was to find that most of the house-party had gathered in one of the Salons.

They were chatting away, trying to decide what they would do in the afternoon.

"I am sure César will have a plan for amusing us," one of the guests exclaimed.

She was a very beautiful young woman with a distinguished husband who was many years older than herself.

As she spoke, Yursa suddenly found herself aware that the lady was thinking now that Zelée de Salône had gone, she herself might have a chance of captivating the *Duc*.

54

Because such an idea shocked Yursa, and she was also shocked at herself for thinking such a thing, she moved away from the circle of the ladies.

She crossed the room to look at a picture.

It was then she asked herself how she could have known what the lady was thinking.

Suddenly she knew that her perception was working so that she could read the thoughts not just of one particular person, as she had sometimes been able to do in the past, but of almost everybody who was staying in the *Château*.

She had learned, without even realising it, that one of the *Duc*'s guests, a middle-aged man who looked as though he drank a great deal, was considering if he could touch his host for a large amount of money.

Another man, who was standing near them, was planning how he could sell the *Duc* a horse for much more than it was worth.

'How can I know... these things? How can... I?' she asked herself.

And yet in some strange way they came into her mind and she knew, however much she tried to reject them, they were true.

'I will think about something else,' she told herself, staring with unseeing eyes at an exquisite picture by Poussin.

It was then, almost as if she could see her standing beside her, that she was aware of Zelée de Salône.

She could feel her hatred reaching out towards her, and she could see the flashing of her eyes and the movement of her lips.

With a little cry which she strangled in her throat she knew she was being cursed.

As fear streaked through her like forked lightning, Yursa knew she must have help.

She glanced at the clock and realised there was still half-an-hour before luncheon would be announced.

Without saying anything, she slipped from the room and down the corridor which she knew led to the side of the *Château* where, as she had seen as she arrived, there was a Chapel.

Because she was so frightened, Yursa sped down the long empty passages hung with fine pictures to where she thought the entrance to the Chapel would be.

She had a good sense of direction and she was not mistaken.

She found an ancient door which opened into a small court-yard.

She was not surprised to see on the other side of it an open door surmounted by a cross.

She entered and found as she expected a small and beautiful Chapel which she could see from its architecture must have been built in the 15th century.

The walls were very thick and the pillars massive.

Behind the altar was a stained glass window containing the heraldic shields of the *Ducs* de Montvéal.

There were several small statues in front of which were burning lighted candles, one being an effigy of Joan of Arc, and Yursa sank down on her knees in front of it.

She felt Joan would understand what she was feeling.

Perhaps she, too, had been frightened when she first heard her voices, and knew they were something which did not come just from herself.

"Help . . . me," Yursa prayed. "Help me . . . because I am . . . afraid! And save me from anything . . . evil which might . . . hurt me!"

She prayed insistently, shutting her eyes, and yet at the same time very conscious of the statue above her.

Then she was aware that the hatred she had felt coming towards her from Zelée de Salône was fading.

It was moving away, almost like a cloud moving before the sun, until at last it had gone.

Yursa drew a deep breath.

"Thank you . . . thank you!" she said.

She knew that she had been blessed and what had threatened her had been removed.

She rose to her feet, knowing she must go back.

"I have no money with me," she said softly, "but later I will come and light a candle to You, and thank You again for helping me."

She genuflected before the altar, crossed herself with the Holy Water which was by the door, then, hurrying across the small court-yard, started to run back the way she had come.

She had just reached the centre of the *Château* where the Salon was situated, when she almost bumped into someone coming out of a door into the corridor.

It was the *Duc*, and he looked at her in surprise.

She was breathless from the speed at which she had run.

Her hair, which she had tidied carefully before she came downstairs, was now curling around her forehead.

"I am sorry . . . I am sorry . . . *Monsieur!*" Yursa gasped.

"Where are you going in such a hurry?" he demanded.

"I . . . I have been to the . . . Chapel."

He looked surprised, and Yursa said:

"It is very beautiful . . . and very . . . Holy."

"Is that what you found?"

She nodded.

Then, as she was aware that his eyes were on her, she put up her hands to tidy her hair.

"I was . . . hurrying," she explained, "in case I was . . . late for . . . luncheon."

"You have a few minute to spare," the *Duc* said with a smile.

He turned and they walked very slowly down the corridor.

They had almost reached the Salon before Yursa said:

"Please . . . you will not . . . say where I have . . . been?"

"Are you ashamed of it?"

"No . . . of course not . . . it is just that I had a . . . reason for going . . . and I do not want . . . anybody to ask . . . questions."

As she spoke she thought she was being very foolish.

Why should anybody ask any questions?

Although her reason for going there had seemed very real to her, not only would no one be likely to understand, but they would also think she was being over-dramatic or deliberately drawing attention to herself.

The *Duc* stopped still and inevitably Yursa did the same.

"Did you go to the Chapel because you were frightened?" he asked in a low voice.

There seemed to be no point in lying, and she told the truth.

"Yes . . . but I am all right . . . now."

"Was it *Madame* de Salône who frightened you?"

Yursa twisted her fingers together and turned her eyes up to his.

"Please . . . do not ask any . . . questions! I know you will . . . not believe me."

"Why should I not believe somebody whom I am quite certain never tells a lie?"

It was a compliment, but Yursa did not realise it.

Instead, she said:

"I am not . . . frightened now."

"And you think it was your prayers in the Chapel which swept away your fears?"

"I . . . I prayed to . . . Joan of Arc."

"Why to her particularly?"

"Because I thought . . . she would . . . understand."

"Then your fear was in some way connected with your voices," the *Duc* said as if he had worked out some complicated mathematical sum.

Yursa nodded, but she did not speak.

"I told you to forget her!" he said sharply.

"I tried . . . but I . . . felt her and I knew . . ."

Yursa stopped, knowing she was about to say too much and he certainly would not understand.

"What did you know?" he asked.

"Please..."

She looked up as she pleaded with him, then as her eyes met his she knew that she must tell him the truth.

He held her captive in a way that made it impossible to withstand him.

She could no more hold out against him than turn back the tide or prevent the moon from shining.

"She... she was... cursing me!" she whispered.

Her voice was so low that he could hardly hear it.

Then as she saw the sudden anger in his eyes and the sharp line to his mouth she added quickly:

"But now I am... safe. Her... vibrations have gone... and perhaps they will... not be able to... come back!"

"We must make sure that they do not!" the *Duc* said in a determined voice.

Then, as if there were nothing more to say, he walked on with Yursa beside him to the Salon.

*   *   *

Luncheon was an entertaining meal with the gentlemen telling stories about their horses and the women striving in every way to amuse the *Duc*.

It was, Yursa thought, as if because Zelée de Salône had gone, they were determined that he should not miss her.

They complimented, teased, and flirted with him with the expertise that was peculiarly French, and certainly put him in a good humour.

60

The food was delicious, and when luncheon was over the *Duc* said:

"I thought this afternoon it would interest you to visit the Palace of the Dukes in Dijon and also, if we have time, see the Tomb of Philip the Bold."

Everybody exclaimed that that would be delightful, but as the *Duc* spoke, he looked at Yursa and knew by the radiance in her eyes how much the idea appealed to her.

She had the feeling that it was something he had planned particularly for her.

Then she told herself that was ridiculous and rebuked herself for being conceited.

They set off in a cavalcade of smart Chaises and open carriages.

The *Duc* had asked the *Marquise* if she would drive with him, and Yursa could not help a little twinge of regret that she could not be his companion.

However, on the return journey he said as they were leaving the Town:

"I think my youngest and most recent guest should accompany me as we return to the *Château*."

Yursa felt a little thrill go through her because he had invited her to be with him.

But she told herself he was just being kind and making sure she was no longer frightened as she had been early that morning.

They had seen the Ducal Palace with its two towers, one named after Philip the Good, while the other, the *Duc* said, was called *Le Tour de Bar*.

It had been the prison of "Good King René," Count of Provence, King of Sicily, and Duke of Bar and Lorraine, and was named after him.

That, unfortunately, was all that was left of the old Palace, and the present one had been built on the order of Louis XIV.

Yursa was entranced by everything, including the magnificent Ducal Tombs in the *Salle de Garde* on the first floor.

Here she was able to see a sculpture of Philip the Bold.

She was, however, even more delighted to look at "the cowled weepers," beautifully carved mourning figures in the little niches on the sides of his tomb.

They wept eternally, she was told, for the man who had fought so many wars for Burgundy.

Because the *Duc* could explain knowledgeably what they were looking at, Yursa felt as if she were hearing one of the stories her grandmother had told her when she was a child.

She had no idea that he was talking entirely to her, since he knew what he was saying was boring most of the other women.

He was well aware all they wanted was that he should talk about himself or gossip.

Like any story-teller, he was flattered by the rapt attention Yursa gave him, and the expressions he could see flitting over her face as she reacted to what he was saying.

Driving home behind a pair of exceptionally fine horses, the *Duc* asked:

"Have you enjoyed your hours of sight-seeing?"

"It was wonderful!" Yursa said. "Like the *Château*, it was exactly what I wanted to find in Burgundy."

"So you have not been disappointed?"

"How could I be when you have been so kind?" she replied.

There was a twist to the *Duc's* lips as he replied:

"That is not an adjective which is usually applied to me."

"Why not?"

"Because many people say I am unkind."

He was thinking, as he spoke, of the women he had left because they bored him.

They were always railing against his cruelty, his unkindness, his selfishness, and his lack of feeling.

Again, because she could follow his thoughts, although fortunately she did not understand exactly what had happened between him and the women he had left, Yursa said:

"My mother used to say that people, because they are greedy, expect too much . . . we should not ask for a present every day of our life."

The *Duc* laughed.

"Your mother was right, and most people, as she must have known, are spoilt."

"If they are spoilt in the way you mean it, then they must be very stupid!"

"Why do you say that?" the *Duc* enquired.

"Because being spoilt means first, that you expect too much; secondly, you are not grateful for what you have already received; and thirdly, you think that you, in particular, must have more and better than anybody else."

The *Duc* considered this as he drove on. Then he said:

"You surprise me, Yursa! Did you think that out for yourself, or did somebody say it to you?"

"I hope I thought it out for myself," Yursa answered. "Living with Nuns makes one realise how completely unselfish they are, so naturally one tries to emulate them."

The *Duc* thought a little cynically that it was something that did not come naturally to everybody, but instead, he said:

"Because you are so young, and not spoilt or blasé, what do you expect of life in the future?"

There was a little pause as Yursa collected her thoughts. Then she said:

"It is not so much what I expect as what I hope and pray for—that I shall be kind and understanding, be able to help those in need, and not hate anybody."

She spoke so simply and with such sincerity that the *Duc* thought that what she had said came from her heart, and it was very touching.

Then, as if he must assert himself, he asked:

"I suppose, like every other woman, you hope to reform those who 'tread the primrose path,' and of course redeem Rakes like myself."

Yursa looked at him in surprise, then unexpectedly her eyes twinkled as she said:

"Do you enjoy being a Rake?"

"Of course!" he replied. "It means I can sample the best things in life without worrying about the consequences!"

"I think the truth is that you are trying to make yourself out to be worse than you are!"

"Why should I do that?"

"Because the need for action is in your blood. As you cannot fight private wars like the ancient *Duc* we have just seen, and because you are too intelligent to 'tilt at windmills,' you have to find a challenge of some sort! Even though you know before you start that you will be the victor!"

The *Duc* turned his head to look at her in surprise.

"Who has been talking to you about me?" he enquired.

Yursa laughed.

"Everybody talks about you, but not in the way I have just said, which, although it may seem impertinent, is my own idea."

"I do not think it is impertinent, but surprising," the *Duc* replied.

They drove on for a little while before he said:

"I suppose what you are really saying is that if I had to fight for something I wanted, as Philip the Bold did, then I would appreciate it more."

"Of course," Yursa agreed, "and it would be a great mistake for you to win too quickly."

The *Duc* thought it was extraordinary that this child, for she was little more, should have identified the reason why he was so often bored.

Although he had, materially, as she knew, everything in his life he could possibly want, everything had been too easy.

"And," he added, "most of the women I pursue surrender all too quickly."

He had often thought that if he had had to fight for a woman he desired, he would appreciate her more.

Unfortunately, they inevitably threw themselves into his arms almost before he knew their names.

But what else was there in life?

To win the races in which his horses were almost invariably first past the winning-post? Bring down a high bird with a single shot? Kill a wild boar with the expertise in which he excelled?

Then he told himself he was being absurd.

How could any man not be content and perfectly happy when he enjoyed a unique social position, and was the possessor of not only a great fortune but much of the finest land in Burgundy?

"Think how, like Napoléon, you would . . . miss it if it . . . was not . . . there," Yursa said in a low voice.

The *Duc* stared at her in sheer astonishment.

"You are reading my thoughts!" he exclaimed incredulously.

She gave a little start and looked at him apprehensively.

"I am sorry . . . I am very sorry," she said. "I did not mean to intrude. It is just that I . . . found I knew what . . . you were . . . thinking."

"How is that possible? How can you do such a thing—and why?"

He spoke sharply because he was startled, and after a moment she said in a low and humble voice:

"I do not . . . think you will . . . believe me, but it is something I have been able to do ever since . . . I came to the *Château* . . . not only with you, but with . . . many of your . . . guests."

"You think you can read their thoughts? I do not believe it!" the *Duc* snapped.

Yursa did not answer but only looked away, and after a moment he said in a kinder voice:

"Forgive me, I should not have spoken like that if you had not startled me. Are you telling me truthfully on everything you hold sacred that you can read not only my thoughts, but those of my friends?"

"Not . . . all of them," Yursa stammered, "and I did not . . . try to do so. It is . . . just that I became . . . aware before luncheon of what one lady was . . . thinking, then . . . what was in the minds of . . . two of the gentlemen."

"Tell me what you know."

"One of the gentlemen was . . . wondering if you would . . . lend him quite a large sum of money."

"And the other?"

"Was planning to . . . sell you a horse."

The *Duc*, who could instantly put a name to both the men mentioned, drove on.

He could hardly believe what he had heard.

He realised from the way Yursa spoke and her embarrassment, that she did not mean to pry into the private thoughts of the two men she had mentioned.

Because he was curious, he could not help asking:

"What was the lady thinking?"

He saw the colour deepen in Yursa's cheeks and knew without her telling him what she had sensed.

Because she was so shy and, he knew, embarrassed, he felt he was being rather cruel.

"I will not tease you any further," he said. "But it is going to be difficult for me to tell my guests to lock up their minds and thoughts when you are about!"

Yursa gave a little laugh, as he intended her to do.

Then, as they began climbing through the woods up to the *Château*, she told herself that she must be very careful in future not to listen to what her voices told her.

She was sure it was only because the *Château*, and, of course, the *Duc*, were unique.

chapter four

THE next morning Yursa rode with the *Duc*, but this time they were accompanied by two of his men-friends.

They complimented her on her riding and her appearance with an eloquence which made her feel embarrassed.

She thought when they returned home that it had been far more amusing when she had ridden alone with the *Duc*.

Then he talked of so many things that had interested her about the country.

There was no time for private conversation before a number of the guests wished to visit the hothouses, and Yursa went with them.

She was delighted with the orchids, which came from many different parts of the world.

Huge masses of malmaison carnations scented

the air long before they entered the glasshouses in which they were being grown.

She was very interested, too, in the Herb Garden, which she was told had existed at Montvéal for over three centuries.

There were so many other things to look at that it was time for luncheon long before Yursa had seen them all.

After the meal was over, her grandmother told her she was taking her to meet the *Duc*'s mother.

The *Duchesse Dovairière* was more or less an invalid and never left her own house, which was about two miles away.

It was a beautiful *Château* surrounded by a formal garden which, with its little box hedges and symmetrical flower-beds was, Yursa thought, like an intricate carpet.

The *Duc*'s mother was, as she expected, a very beautiful old lady.

She held out her hands in delight when she saw Yursa, exclaiming as she did so:

"You are very like your mother!"

Yursa sat beside her while she talked about her mother and when she had visited England as a young girl.

A little later she suggested to Yursa that she might like to explore the *Château*, and she was tactful enough to realise that she wished to talk to her grandmother alone.

She therefore went off eagerly to look at the beautifully furnished rooms and the pictures that she was knowledgeable enough to realise were exceptionally fine examples of French art.

As soon as she had gone, the *Duchesse* said:

"She is perfect! What does César think of her?"

Lady Helmsdale realised the eagerness with which the *Duchesse* spoke, and replied:

"I honestly do not know, Yvonne. He is always enigmatic, but at least that woman has left the *Château*."

"So I was told," the *Duchesse* said, "but I keep asking myself for how long?"

"I am sure," Lady Helmsdale said slowly, "that César is intelligent enough to be aware why I have brought Yursa with me to France."

"I spoke to him before you arrived," the *Duchesse* said, "and he told me firmly and categorically that he had no intention of marrying again. In fact, it was a subject he did not wish to discuss!"

She paused, then she said:

"But, I must tell you in confidence, I have heard that Zelée de Salône is determined to be his wife!"

Lady Helmsdale sighed.

"I suppose that is something we might have expected. But surely he will not be so foolish?"

"How can we know? How can we tell what goes on in César's mind?" his mother asked despondently. "I love my son, and I want him to be happy, which I am sure he will never be with that unpleasant, evil woman."

"What makes you think she is evil?" Lady Helmsdale asked. "It is a word you have used before, and I have since wondered what you know to brand her in such an appalling way."

"It is difficult to put into words," the *Duchesse* replied, "but the servants are all terrified of her, and

71

speak of her in a manner which tells me they know a great deal more than they will say."

"About what?"

"I wish I knew! If I did, I would tell César, although I doubt if he would listen to me."

"It seems strange," Lady Helmsdale persisted, "that the word 'evil' should be applied to any woman unless there is a reason for it."

She thought for a moment before she added:

"She, of course, looks fantastic, and has a sinister serpentine grace which is accentuated by her upturned eyes, but it must be more than that."

"It is!" the *Duchesse* agreed. "When I speak of her, even to the oldest servants, who have been with me for years and have known César since he was in the cradle, their eyes flicker and the words I want to hear will not come from their lips."

"It is certainly very strange!" Lady Helmsdale said, "and I know that if only César would realise it, Yursa would make him a perfect wife."

Her voice softened as she went on:

"She is sweet, gentle, and as she has seen nothing ugly or unpleasant in her life, she is pure and, of course, very innocent."

"Just what I want in a daughter-in-law," the *Duchesse* sighed.

"We can only pray that in the next few days César will realise Yursa's good qualities," Lady Helmsdale said, "and forget Zelée de Salône's very existence."

"She will do everything in her power to prevent him from doing that!" the *Duchesse* murmured.

There was a note almost like despair in her voice.

72

Driving back to the *Château,* Yursa made her grandmother tell her more than she knew already about
the history of Burgundy.

She listened with the same rapt attention she had
given the *Duc*.

As a compliment to his English visitors, the *Duc*
had ordered tea to be served in the Orangery.

Lady Helmsdale was delighted with the excellent
China tea that was provided, while Yursa enjoyed the
pâtisseries.

A number of the French guests joined them and
agreed that English tea was an excellent meal and
that it seemed a pity it was not popular in France.

The *Duc* did not appear, and after tea Yursa visited the Picture Gallery in which she had previously
spent very little time.

Now she could have a closer look at the collection
which was, she had learnt, one of the finest in the
whole of France.

She found herself wishing that the *Duc* was with her,
then she wondered if because they had not seen him
since luncheon he had gone to visit Zelée de Salône.

Even to think of the woman who had cursed her
made her shiver and feel as if she did not want to be
alone.

She therefore went to her bed-room earlier than
usual to find Jeanne already there, laying out her
gown for the evening.

"As there's a smaller party to-night than usual,
M'mselle," she said, "I thought you might wear this

73

rather more simple gown, which at the same time is very pretty."

It was a young girl's gown that the Dowager had brought from Paris.

While it was deceptively simple, it had a *chic* and an elegance that was undeniably French.

Because Yursa was young, the bustle was very small and consisted of little more than a large satin bow from which cascaded out a multitude of tiny frills.

The front of the gown was draped in a manner that had been introduced by Frederick Worth.

It made her look like a young Greek goddess and the small puffed sleeves and draped bodice left her neck and shoulders bare.

As she had no jewelery, Jeanne tied a narrow piece of velvet ribbon round her long neck.

She attached to it one of the perfect little star orchids which was among those Yursa had brought back from the glasshouses.

"*Vous êtes très belle, M'mselle!*" Jeanne exclaimed, "and we've been saying below stairs that no young lady as beautiful as you has ever stayed here!"

"Thank you," Yursa said shyly. "You are very kind to me, Jeanne, and I like having you to look after me."

"You must take care of yourself *M'mselle*," Jeanne said, "and pray that your Guardian Angel will watch over you."

"I am sure he is doing that already," Yursa replied.

As she spoke she thought of how her prayers in the Chapel had swept away the evil of Zelée de Salône, which had never returned.

Because she had a sudden qualm that it might, she said:

74

"Pray for me, Jeanne . . . I need your prayers!"

"I do that already, *M'mselle*," Jeanne replied. "I pray, and so do many others in the *Château* who love the *Duc* and want his happiness."

Yursa knew exactly what Jeanne meant.

For a moment she was surprised that the servants should be aware that there was an ulterior motive for her grandmother bringing her to France.

Then she told herself with a little smile that nothing could be kept from the knowledge of those who listened and served.

It was something that had often made her mother laugh.

She remembered her father had questioned how it was that the staff should know about something private of which he was hardly himself aware.

Her mother had explained:

"Dearest Edward, in a household even the walls have ears! It is known in the Servants' Hall what is happening long before it reaches the Dining-Room!"

Her father had laughed, but it was something Yursa had found true with her Nurses and Governesses, besides the Butler and the footmen who waited on them.

There was no point in her feeling embarrassed.

The servants in the *Château* who loved the *Duc* thought of her as a prospective bride who had come "on approval" for him to see if she was suitable.

And although it might seen undignified, that was exactly the case.

As she went down the stairs, the *Duc* appeared in the hall, coming from the corridor where his Study was situated.

He looked up and saw her and waited until she came down the last steps to join him.

"You have had a good day?" he enquired.

"I went with Grandmama to meet your mother, *la Duchesse*."

"And I am sure," the *Duc* said with a twinkle in his eye, "that she told you what a splendid person I was!"

Yursa laughed.

"How can you imagine she would say anything else?"

"I assure you when we are alone she is very strict and very critical, but to the outside world she is whole-heartedly my supporter."

He was smiling as he spoke and Yursa thought that whatever he had been doing, it had put him in a very good temper.

Then, as he opened the Drawing-Room door, she could not help worrying if, in fact, he had been with Zelée de Salône and, whatever his relatives might say, that he was determined to keep her in his life.

The *Duc* had, as it happened, been inspecting one of his vineyards.

It was some distance from the *Château*, and there was trouble with the Overseer.

Because he did not wish to rebuke the man with anybody else present, he had ridden there alone.

He found, however, that things were not as bad as he had expected, and, in fact, what had been wrong had already been corrected.

The Overseer had shown him some new developments which pleased him, and he had learnt that they could expect an exceptionally good harvest later in the year.

He had ridden home knowing that the same conditions applied to his other vineyards, thinking that 1865 might be an exceptional year for wine.

He decided that if it were, he would certainly be richer than he was already!

The idea made him think of a number of ways in which he would be able to spend the money.

One would be to buy for the *Château* two pictures which he had coveted for some time.

They were, however, enormously expensive and he had hesitated to spend so much money.

Dinner was as delicious as usual, but, while the card-tables had been set out in the Salon, a number of the *Duc*'s guests said they did not intend to play, as they wished to go to bed early.

Several of them were leaving in the morning to return to their homes in other parts of France.

A distinguished Ambassador and his wife were going to Paris.

They therefore sat around talking until while it was still comparatively early, a number of the ladies decided to say good-night and go to bed.

As her grandmother was amongst them, Yursa went, too, to find when she entered her bed-room that Jeanne was not there.

She did not ring for the maid but went to the window to pull back the curtains.

There was a full moon, and the sky seemed ablaze with stars.

She looked, as she had before, over the valley and thought that nothing could be more beautiful.

In the moonlight she could see the shining silver of the rivers and distinguish the distant towers of Dijon.

There were many more twinkling lights than there had been the other evening.

She heard a faint knock on her door and, thinking it was Jeanne, called out: "Come in!"

The door opened and she said without turning round:

"Do come and look at the moonlight, Jeanne. It is impossible to think that anything could be more lovely!"

Jeanne did not answer and Yursa turned her head to see a strange maid.

"I thought you were Jeanne!" she exclaimed. "Is she off duty?"

"*Non, M'mselle,* but she's hurt herself, and she asks if you'll come and see her."

"But, of course!" Yursa said. "Has she had an accident?"

"A small one, *M'mselle,* but her hands are bleeding, and she thought you would know what to do."

"I will come at once," Yursa said. "Have you any bandages?"

"*Oui, M'mselle,* everything. If you'll just come and see her..."

Yursa walked to the door and the maid hurried ahead.

She led her quickly along the broad corridor and down a small staircase which Yursa had not seen before.

Then they walked along a narrow passage and down some more stairs which were dimly lit, unlike the rest of the *Château*, which always seemed to be a blaze of light.

Yursa thought vaguely that it was in the direction of the Chapel, but she did not recognise it.

When they had descended the last staircase, they were in what seemed a small, very dark hall with an outer door in it.

She wondered if Jeanne had not fallen inside the *Château*, as she had assumed, but outside.

Yursa was just about to ask if that was true, when the maid opened the door.

She thought she saw somebody large, like a man, in darkness, but was not certain.

Whoever it was pushed through the door, bumping into her, and something dark and heavy was thrown over her head.

She gave a cry of protest, but her voice was lost in the thickness of the material which covered her.

Then she was picked up and carried outside.

She was put down roughly on what she thought was a wooden floor.

But as she struggled ineffectively she felt the floor beneath her move and there was the sound of wheels and of horses' hoofs.

She realised that she was in a cart.

Because what covered her was so thick and heavy, her voice as she tried to cry out for help was lost, and she doubted if even those nearby could hear her.

She felt hands on her ankles and realised that her feet were being tied together; then a rope enveloped her waist and pinned her arms to her sides.

The cart was very uncomfortable and she was

thrown from side to side as the horses gathered speed.

She was aware that somebody was sitting near her, and even if she had struggled to be free she could not escape.

No one spoke and there was no sound except the rumble of wheels over stony ground and the clatter of the horses' hoofs.

'I have been . . . kidnapped!' Yursa told herself.

There was no need to ask who was responsible for such an outrage.

She might have guessed, she thought, that when Zelée de Salône's curses failed, she would try to hurt her in some more violent way.

Yursa was frightened, so frightened that she felt as if her heart might stop beating.

Then, because there was nothing else she could do, she began to pray to her Guardian Angel as Jeanne had told her to do.

"Help . . . me! Help . . . me! Save . . . me!" she begged.

Remembering the hatred in Zelée de Salône's eyes and the vibrations which had emanated from her, she was desperately afraid.

They must have travelled for perhaps fifteen minutes, although it seemed longer.

The horses, because of the rough ground over which they were travelling, had to go much slower and still slower, until they were moving at a walk.

Suddenly, the cart came to a standstill, and now Yursa could hear voices, women's voices.

It seemed, although it was hard to hear through the thickness of the material which covered her head, that they were intoning, or, rather, chanting in what seemed to be a strange, incomprehensible language.

Then strong arms were lifting her out from the cart.

Somebody untied her feet and, when the rope was taken from her waist, the covering was lifted from her head.

For a moment, because she had been in complete darkness, and also because she was afraid, she could see nothing.

Then there was the light of flares, and she could see she was in a wood.

There were also several people near to her, although she was not aware of them for a few seconds, and they were all women.

They were looking at her, staring at her.

In the light of the flares which were coming nearer she could see they were peasant-women, dressed in the worn gowns they worked in in the fields, but with their hair falling loose over their shoulders.

She thought they were young, but it was difficult to see clearly until a flaming torch carried by another woman lit up the scene.

It was then because the sounds of those around her were so eerie that Yursa asked:

"Why . . . am I . . . here? Why have you . . . brought . . . me away from . . . the *Château* in this . . . disgraceful . . . manner?"

She meant her voice to ring out, but because she was afraid, it was low and, she thought, rather childlike.

The women looking at her did not reply, but the woman near her holding the torch took a step to one side.

Confronting her was Zelée de Salône!

Her appearance was very different from the way she had looked when she was at the *Château*.

Now her dark hair which had been dressed so fashionably was flowing over her, and she wore a peculiar dress which flared out at the knees.

Her shoulders and arms were bare except for the skin of a wild animal which hung down from one shoulder over one breast, and was caught round her waist with a gold band.

She wore golden earrings which flashed as her head moved.

There were bracelets on her wrists and, Yursa was to notice later, round her ankles, above her bare feet.

She stood looking at Yursa, and now the vibrations of hatred seemed to pour out from her so that Yursa felt as if she could not only feel but see them.

With an effort, because she had the idea that Zelée de Salône was trying to hypnotise her, she asked:

"Why have...you brought...me here, *Madame?*"

"I should have thought that was obvious," Zelée replied. "I warned you, but you would not listen to my warning! Now you must pay the price for your disobedience to our Lord and Master!"

She spoke with a strange exaltation in her voice.

Yursa saw in the light of the flare she held that the pupils of her eyes were dilated and very dark.

"You had no . . . right to carry me . . . away!" Yursa managed to say.

Zelée laughed, and it was a very unpleasant sound.

"To-night I have every right," she said. "I am a servant of Satan, and when he calls, you obey! To-night, you insignificant Englishwoman, you have the honour to be the sacrifice to our Master! He will then give us the power we are asking of him."

As she spoke, still in that strange, wild tone, there was a murmur of excitement from the women who were listening.

Now Zelée turned round with a swirl of her skirt, and without being told Yursa was seized by the arms and forced to follow her.

They went farther into the wood, where there was a clearing, and Yursa could see more flares and more women and knew without being told that this was a Witches' Sabbat.

She felt a shiver at the idea, but there was nothing she could do but march along behind Zelée.

Then, as she appeared, the women who had been intoning as Yursa had heard them all rose to their feet.

Zelée stopped.

"She is here!" she screamed. "Here, the sacrifice that our Lord Satan, Prince of Darkness, has demanded. We have brought him what you all know he desired, an Englishwoman to pay the price for the crime the English perpetrated against our own Joan of Arc."

The women cheered in a way that made them sound as if they were screaming.

Then as they pressed forward to look at Yursa, Zelée said:

"Do not let us waste any time, but offer her up so that she dies as Joan died, in the flames, for which Burgundy has wept tears of blood."

Listening to her and the strange wildness in her voice, it suddenly struck Yursa that she was doped in some way.

She remembered vaguely hearing that the herbs that Witches used in their potions often included wild poppy, which yielded opium.

Then as Zelée moved away, Yursa could see directly in front of her there was a post in the centre of the clearing.

She knew as her captors pushed her forward that she was to be tied to it, and only as she reached it did the full horror of what was to take place sweep over her.

She had to climb over several stacked logs to reach the post; then they turned her round and wound a rope around her waist.

Another was tied round her feet, and she understood with a terror that was almost beyond thought that she was to be burned at the stake!

Zelée was screaming and chattering, and the Witches, most of them young, rather stupid-looking women with their long hair falling untidily round their faces, were rummaging about in the wood.

They came back with small branches of dried leaves, throwing them on top of the logs that had been arranged round the post.

It seemed to Yursa that she was in a bad dream from which she could not wake up.

It was impossible to believe that this was really happening to her.

Could Zelée de Salône, whom she had seen as an elegantly dressed social guest in the *Château*, be this wild, drugged, screaming creature?

Yet there was no doubt that she was mad with excitement and the effect of the drugs she had taken.

Zelée kept looking at Yursa, who pressed her lips together, and lifted her chin defiantly, because she knew what satisfaction it would give if she begged for mercy.

Suddenly, as if her hatred welled up within her, Zelée screamed:

"Why should she burn in a gown when Joan died in little more than her shift? Take it from her! Cut it off! Pull it off! Let her look like the English *canaille* she is!"

Two women hurried to obey her.

They dragged the drapery from Yursa's bodice and the delicately puffed sleeves which covered the tops of her arms.

Another woman hacked away at the pretty bustle and the draped skirt, until Yursa wore nothing but her chemise.

Only the petticoat which hung from her waist covered her legs.

The women flung the pieces of the gown they had ripped away onto the logs, and other women coming from between the trees covered them with more leaves and twigs.

"Pull down her hair!" Zelée shouted.

Roughly, so that Yursa winced, but forced herself not to cry out, two women snatched away the pins with which Jeanne had arranged her hair.

It fell over her shoulders, covering, she thought, a little of her nakedness.

"That is better!" Zelée sneered. "Now she is an ordinary creature of whom nobody could be afraid! She will be humiliated and destroyed! Like the English brutes and murderers who killed our Joan!"

The name obviously meant something to the young Witches, who repeated it to themselves as if it were a catch-phrase and shouted and cheered after everything that Zelée said.

Drawing herself up, she cried:

"That is enough! Now we will begin to invoke the Great One, our Master the King, He in whom we believe, ask for His Presence here amongst us to-night."

"Our Master—Beelzebub! Adrameleeh! Lucifer! Satan, we are thy slaves! Come to us! Come! Come! Honour us with thy presence!"

The women intoned the words, but now there was nothing low or melodious about their voices.

Instead, they were shrill, some of them shrieking, several waving their hands as they did so.

"We worship you!" Zelée was calling. "We worship you, Satan! We are your slaves, your lovers! We kneel at your feet! Hear our cry and come to us!"

"Come to us! Come to us! Lord, we worship you!"

The women's voices rose to a shrill crescendo.

As she listened, the rope which held Yursa's feet

and hands seemed to bite into her flesh.

She could feel the evil behind every word and pulsating in every breath they drew.

Then she looked away from them up into the sky towards the stars.

She knew that God would hear her prayer and that if she died, it would not be Satan who had carried her away, but God.

She had prayed every night ever since she was a child, and she felt her mother was with Him now.

There was no chance of her being saved, she thought, but at least she would die knowing that death was unimportant.

She belonged to everything that was good and beautiful, and therefore Satan could have no claim on her.

She felt as if her whole being strained upwards toward the stars and that the Saints were protecting her, and she could see her mother's face.

"Help me, Mama," she prayed. "Help me to be brave, so that I do not scream or humiliate myself before these terrible women!"

She thought her mother smiled at her.

Then once again she was hearing Zelée's words above the noise of the other women.

"Come, Satan, come! Beelzebub, hear us! We are waiting! Here is your sacrifice! Here is the English-woman who will die in your name!"

Then, taking her eyes from the stars and looking down, Yursa saw Zelée seize the torch from the woman nearest to her and bend forward.

She ignited the leaves and twigs at the base of the pile.

As she did so, Yursa was aware that she was thinking that the slower the fire burned before it reached her, the more frightening it would be and the more pain it would cause her.

Slowly, Zelée walked all round the pile, making the twigs and the dried leaves burn up sharply and just begin to affect the bottom row of the logs.

The smoke from it began to rise.

Yursa thought that if she breathed deeply, perhaps it would dull her consciousness and help her to bear the pain when it came, when the flames reached her feet and legs.

"Help me. Oh, God, help me!" she prayed.

She looked up again at the stars, feeling that only they could see what was happening to her and in some way would help her.

"Help me! Help me!"

Now the bottom row of the logs were ignited.

Zelée gave out a command and the Witches, joining hands, began to dance round the burning pile.

They were still shouting, crying out their prayers to Satan, and the logs were beginning to crackle.

Yursa knew it was only a question of minutes before she would begin to burn.

"God, help me!"

There was nothing else she could say as even the words of her prayers slipped from her mind.

She was left with an intensity that consumed her whole mind, heart, and soul for the God in which she believed.

Then, as the women's voices rose higher and higher, Zelée screamed with ecstasy:

"He is here! Satan is here!"

Yursa found herself trembling.

Could they really have summoned Satan by their faith in him?

chapter five

WHEN all his older guests had gone up to bed, the *Duc* found himself left with three of his friends who were about the same age as himself.

"What shall we do?" he asked. "Do you feel like a game of Bridge?"

"I have a better idea," one man replied. "I would like to see a duel between you and Henri. It is something I always enjoy."

The *Duc* laughed, but Henri, the *Vicomte* Soisson, said ruefully:

"That means that, as usual, I shall be defeated!"

"You can at least try," his friend said, laughing, "but perhaps we should handicap César by blind-folding him."

"You will do nothing of the sort!" the *Duc* answered. "Let us go to the Armoury and choose our foils."

Laughing, the four men went down the corridor.

They had almost reached the Armoury which was one of the most interesting rooms in the *Château*, when there were footsteps behind them.

The *Duc* turned and saw Jeanne, Yursa's maid, hurrying towards him.

"*Monseigneur!* I must speak to you, *Monseigneur!*"

The *Duc's* three friends went into the Armoury while he asked somewhat irritably:

"What is it? You are Jeanne, are you not?"

"*Oui, Monseigneur,*" Jeanne replied.

She dropped him a little curtsy, and he realised she was very agitated.

"Well, what is it you want?"

"It is *M'mselle*—*Monseigneur*—they have—taken her!"

The *Duc* looked at her in bewilderment.

"Taken *Mademoiselle?* What are you talking about?"

For a moment Jeanne seemed tongue-tied, then she crossed herself and said in a whisper he could hardly hear:

"It is the—Witches' Sabbat!"

The *Duc* was suddenly very still.

"The Witches' Sabbat?" he said angrily. "What are you telling me?"

"They have taken *M'mselle* to it, *Monseigneur*. I was deliberately—detained downstairs and when I —escaped I saw the new maid who I suspected as being—one of—them taking *M'mselle* down the Cardinal's Staircase."

The *Duc* was listening, but he found it hard to believe what he was hearing.

Jeanne gave a little sob and continued:

"I watched them—I watched them from the top of the stairs, *Monseigneur,* and they threw a—blanket over *M'mselle's* head—and carried her to where there was—a cart waiting—outside."

The *Duc* drew in his breath.

Then, as Jeanne looked up at him pleadingly, the tears on her cheeks, he knew she was trembling, and he asked:

"Where have they taken her?"

"They will—kill me if they—know it was I who— told you the place, *Monseigneur!*"

"I will protect you," the *Duc* said, "but tell me quickly where *Mademoiselle* has been taken."

"To *le Bois du Dragon!*"

The words were only a whisper, and again Jeanne crossed herself.

"Do not be afraid," the *Duc* said. "You were right to tell me."

He went into the Armoury, saying in an urgent tone which surprised his friends:

"Quick! Come with me! There is something evil happening, and we have to prevent it at all costs. We will be riding, but there is no time to change!"

As he spoke he pulled a rapier from where it was hanging on the wall in its case.

Then he started to run down the corridor towards the door which led to the stable, followed by his three friends.

* * *

Smoke was rising around Yursa, and now she could hear the crackle of the twigs and feel the heat on her legs.

She did not look, but turned her face up to the sky, seeing the stars overhead and the moon illuminating everything with its silver light.

The prayers that came from her lips were very simple.

She no longer begged God to save her, knowing it was impossible, but prayed only that she might be brave when her body began to burn.

She thought of Joan of Arc, and knew that she had confounded her English murderers with her bravery, praying with her head turned to the sky until she died.

"Let it be... quick! Please... God, let it be... quick!" Yursa pleaded.

She felt as she prayed that not only was God hearing her, but also that her mother was near her.

Now, as the shrieks and excitement of the women increased, they spoke as though the Devil was with them.

Yursa forced herself not to listen to their hard voices, but to think of the angels who she was sure were with her.

Yet despite every resolution, she heard Zelée's scream:

"The Master is here! Lucifer is with us! He has heard our plea! Our cries have reached him!"

As a tremor of fear swept through Yursa, she closed her eyes.

Now, because she was frightened of seeing Satan, she prayed again.

"Please God . . . save me . . . Holy Mary . . . Mother of God . . . save me! Do not . . . let this evil . . . touch me!"

It was then the heat seemed to intensify and she knew without looking that the logs had caught fire and the flames were beginning to rise.

"Satan! Master! You are with us, and we kneel at your feet!" the women yelled.

Zelée flung out her arms as if she would embrace her lover, crying as she did so:

"Lucifer, Prince of Darkness, My Lord, My Leader, I am yours!"

There were yells of excitement from all the women, and it was their screams which guided the *Duc* towards them.

He swept into the clearing at a gallop, his rapier in his hand, his three friends close behind.

He saw at a glance what was happening and, springing down from his horse, he advanced towards the women who retreated from him in fear.

Then, realising who he was, they started to run as quickly as they could into the darkness of the wood.

Only Zelée stayed, defying him.

He ignored her, starting to kick away the burning logs so that he could reach Yursa.

"You are too late!" she jeered. "She is sacrificed to Satan! Lucifer has taken her and . . ."

Before she could finish the sentence, Henri de Soisson pushed her to one side, almost knocking her over as he realised what the *Duc* was doing.

Then he, too, was kicking away the burning logs, and the other two men did the same.

Their horses were left unattended as they realised there was no time to be lost unless Yursa was to be burnt alive as the Witches had intended.

The *Duc* reached her first.

He cut her bonds with his rapier, and, flinging it to the ground, lifted her into his arms above the flames and carried her to safety.

She was half-suffocated by the smoke.

Bewildered by fear, for a moment she hardly realised she had been saved at the last moment by her prayers and by the mercy of God.

The *Duc* carried her to where the horses were congregated together.

Henri, realising there was no longer any need to continue to put out the flames, caught the *Duc*'s stallion by the bridle.

He lifted Yursa into the saddle and mounted up behind her.

Only when he picked up the reins in his right hand, holding Yursa close against him with his left, did the *Vicomte* ask:

"What shall we do about the other women?"

The *Duc* looked round the clearing, but the only one left was Zelée.

Crouching on the ground where she had been thrown, she was regarding him with fierce dark eyes, like a tigress at bay.

"Leave them!" he replied to the *Vicomte*. "They can do no more harm to-night."

He turned his horse as he spoke and began to ride back through the wood and, after conferring amongst themselves, his three friends followed him.

The *Duc* rode slowly and carefully towards the *Château*, aware that Yursa was semi-conscious after all she had been through.

Her face was hidden against his shoulder, and her golden hair covered the nakedness of her shoulders.

He could see her tattered petticoat where the Witches had torn it, and there were scorch marks on her feet, which he knew would be very painful later.

He was angry with a rage which made his chin square and his lips close in a tight line.

How was it possible that such a thing could happen on his estate and to one of his guests?

They emerged from the wood, and now Montvéal was just ahead of them.

Yursa stirred, and now she spoke in a small voice that he could only just hear.

"You . . . you saved . . . me!"

"With God's help, and the good sense of Jeanne, who saw you being carried away."

"The . . . other maid . . . told me that . . . Jeanne was . . . injured, but then I . . . found that . . . *Madame* meant me to die!"

"I will deal with her later," the *Duc* said. "What you have to do now, Yursa, is try to forget that this ever happened. I promise that nothing like it will ever occur again."

He felt her tremble as she asked:

"How can you . . . be sure of . . . that? She will . . . still want to . . . kill me."

"That is something I will not allow," the *Duc* said, "but you have to trust me."

"I . . . I was . . . frightened!"

"I thought when I saw you looking up at the sky that no woman could be so brave, or so magnificent in such a terrifying situation."

The kindness in his voice, and also the note of admiration percolated through the fog which still seemed to Yursa to chill her mind, so that she could not think clearly.

Then, as if like a child she realised she was safe, even from the Devil himself, she began to cry.

At first it was just tears streaming unchecked from her eyes, then it was like a tempest, shaking her body so that the *Duc* felt her tremble against him.

"It is all right," he said soothingly, "quite all right now, and I swear on everything that is holy that it shall never happen another time."

As he spoke he had the feeling that she could not hear him.

They reached the *Château*, and the grooms who had earlier saddled their horses with a speed which had never been exceeded before, were waiting.

Very slowly the *Duc* managed to dismount, still holding Yursa in his arms.

He carried her up the steps and found as he expected that Jeanne was waiting in the hall.

"You have—saved her, *Monseigneur!* You have— saved her!" she cried.

"It was *you* who saved her!" the *Duc* replied. "But she has suffered cruelly."

As he spoke he began to ascend the stairs, still holding Yursa close against him.

She had stopped crying, but he knew she was clinging to him as if she were afraid.

He reached her bed-room, Jeanne running ahead

to open the door, and carrying her to the bed, he laid her down gently.

She gave a little murmur of protest as if she could not bear him to leave her, and he said quietly:

"Jeanne will look after you, and I will come back when she has bandaged your feet and got you into bed."

He was not certain whether Yursa understood.

She was looking at him with eyes that seemed to plead with him, her long eye-lashes still wet with tears.

He thought by the light of the candles that she looked exceedingly lovely.

But he realised, too, that she was in a state of shock after what had happened to her.

He left her with Jeanne and went down the stairs to find that his friends, as he expected, had gone into the Salon and each of them held a glass of champagne in his hand.

As he joined them the *Vicomte* said:

"If I had not seen it with my own eyes, César, I would not have believed such a thing could happen in a civilised world!"

"Witches still exist in all countries," the *Duc* replied, "but it is the first time I have known a Sabbat to take place on my land!"

There was no doubt of the fury in his voice as he spoke.

One of his other friends handed him a glass of champagne, and said:

"Well, thank God, you saved that lovely girl! What are you going to do about *Madame* de Salône?"

"What can I do?" the *Duc* asked.

He took a sip of his champagne and said:

"I think we are all sensible enough to be aware that the less said about this the better."

His friends nodded agreement as he went on:

"I am going to ask you to give me your word of honour that you will not speak to anybody, and I mean anybody, of what has occurred here to-night."

For a moment they all looked at him in surprise. Then Henri de Soisson replied:

"You are right, César, of course! It would be a great mistake and very damaging to Lady Yursa if people talked, or the newspapers got hold of the story."

"That is what I was thinking," the *Duc* agreed. "And of one thing we can all be certain, the servants will keep silent. They are far too frightened of offending the Witches!"

"But it was a maid who told you that Lady Yursa had been taken away," Henri remarked.

"She will not talk," the *Duc* said. "Because she was brave enough to save Lady Yursa, she will be too frightened of any repercussions if it were known that it was she who told me where they had taken her."

"I am sure you are right," the *Vicomte* replied.

The *Duc* finished his glass of champagne, then went back to Yursa's bed-room.

Jeanne had undressed her and got her into bed, and the *Duc* had taken upstairs with him a glass which contained a little brandy diluted with water.

He went to the side of the bed, and without speaking put an arm behind Yursa's head.

"I want you to drink this," he said.

She did not protest, but obeyed him like a child.

She drank a little of what was in the glass, then put up her hand.

"Just another sip," the *Duc* coaxed.

He put down the glass and, looking at Jeanne, said:

"I want to speak to you for a moment."

He pressed Yursa's hand and said softly:

"I am coming back."

She seemed to understand, and he went through the communicating door into the *Boudoir* which was attached to Yursa's bed-room.

Jeanne followed him, and he realised as he turned to speak to her that she was looking at him apprehensively.

"I am extremely grateful to you, Jeanne," he said, "and you saved *Mademoiselle's* life."

The maid gave a little gasp and clasped her hands together, but she did not speak and the *Duc* went on:

"I intend to reward you with a sum of money which will enable you to have a large dowry should you wish to be married."

"Thank you, *Monseigneur*," Jeanne replied, "but I am happy to have saved *M'mselle*. It was—wicked that she should be—taken away by those who do not follow—*le Bon Dieu*."

"That is right," the *Duc* agreed. "At the same time, I want you to promise me that you will not speak of it to anybody in the household, or tell your family what has happened. My friends have promised never to speak of it again."

He saw the relief in Jeanne's eyes and knew, as he had suspected, that she was very frightened of the Witches, in case they took their revenge.

"You will understand," he continued, "that I have no wish to send for a doctor or for anybody to ask questions as to what has happened to *Mademoiselle* to-night?"

"I swear to you—*Monseigneur*, that I'll never—speak of it," Jeanne murmured.

"Thank you," the *Duc* replied, "and I am very grateful to you."

He walked back into the bed-room, and Jeanne tactfully did not follow him.

He crossed the room and sat down on the side of the bed, taking Yursa's hand in his.

"It is all over," he said quietly, "and now you have to get well very quickly."

He felt her fingers tremble in his, and he said:

"I have sworn Jeanne and my friends to secrecy, so that no one will know what has occurred. Do you understand that you have to be brave enough to face the world again to-morrow, as if nothing had happened?"

"But . . . it *did* . . . happen!" Yursa whispered.

"Go to sleep," the *Duc* said. "Everything will seem different after a night's rest. To-morrow we will talk about it together."

He smiled at her in a way that most women found irresistible, then, taking her hand, kissed it very gently.

He thought she looked at him in surprise, and he rose to his feet, saying:

"Good-night, Yursa. You know better than I do that your Guardian Angel is watching over you."

With that he left the room.

Yursa shut her eyes as she said in her heart:

"Thank You, God . . . and thank you . . . Mama. I know that you . . . sent him to . . . save me."

*   *   *

The following morning Jeanne told the Dowager that Yursa had passed a sleepless night, and that she had persuaded her to stay in bed.

"A sleepless night?" Lady Helmsdale exclaimed. "That is very unlike my granddaughter."

"I think, *Madame*, perhaps *M'mselle* ate something that disagreed with her," Jeanne said. "There were oysters on the menu at dinner, and although they were fresh, there might have been one amongst them that was bad. It does happen sometimes."

"That is true," Lady Helmsdale conceded. "And tell my granddaughter there is no hurry for her to rise, and if you can persuade her to sleep until luncheon time, so much the better."

"I'll do my best, *Madame*," Jeanne replied, curtsying before she left the room.

*   *   *

Yursa slept for an hour or so, then with an effort she told Jeanne she must get up.

She realised it would be a great mistake for anybody in the house-party to enquire too closely as to why she was unwell.

She thought, too, that the *Duc* might despise her for being cowardly.

He would know, if no one else did, that she was afraid to face the world after what had happened.

She wanted more than anything else to remain

103

unseen and for no one to ask her any awkward questions.

One of her ankles was very sore, and Jeanne bound it up, telling Yursa as she did so that she must say she had a bad mosquito bite.

"It's quite a likely thing to happen, *M'mselle*," she said, "and anyway, we'll find a gown to cover it so that nobody'll notice the bandage."

She helped Yursa to dress in one of the pretty gowns her grandmother had brought her from Paris which was white and trimmed with broderie anglaise.

It had inserts through which was threaded narrow blue velvet ribbon.

There was also a sash of blue velvet to tie round her tiny waist, and as with her other gowns, the bustle was a small one, but very graceful.

As she dressed, Yursa tried not to think of the beautiful gown which the Witches had torn from her body and which had been consumed by the flames.

Even to think of what had occurred made her tremble, and she forced herself to look at the sunshine coming through the windows.

There was a vase of orchids on her dressing-table and roses filled another bowl on a beautifully inlaid commode.

She went down the stairs slowly, holding on to the banisters, but she managed to walk with her head held high into the Salon, where everybody had assembled before luncheon.

Only the *Duc* and his three friends were aware that she was very pale and that there were little dark

lines under her eyes that had not been there yester-
day.

The rest of the party were gossiping amongst
themselves, and as she went to her grandmother's
side, the Dowager asked:

"Are you feeling better, dearest?"

"I am quite all right now, Grandmama," Yursa replied.

"Your maid thought you had eaten something that
disagreed with you."

"I expect that is what it was."

At luncheon the *Duc* noticed that she was making
a great effort to talk to the gentlemen on either side
of her, and thought that no one could be braver, or
more self-composed.

Because he thought it would make it easier for
her, he said that after luncheon, while the others
went driving, he had promised Yursa that he would
show her the Picture Gallery.

"I will tell her the history of some of my pictures,"
he announced.

"Quite frankly, César," one of his lady-guests remarked, "I would prefer to go driving behind two of
your superb horses! I have heard your lectures on
the family treasures before!"

"And quite obviously found them dull!" the *Duc*
retorted.

"Not dull, but somewhat impersonal," the lady replied with a provocative glance.

He laughed.

The Dowager went to her room because she said
she had some letters to write.

When the others had driven away, the *Duc* said to Yursa:

"Before we go to the Picture Gallery, I want to talk to you, and we can do that most comfortably in my Study."

They walked down the corridor to the room which she knew was peculiarly his own.

As he shut the door she moved to the large bow window and sat down on the velvet-covered window-seat.

The sunshine was on her hair, and he thought as he joined her that no one could look more beautiful or, in spite of everything she had suffered, so serene.

He sat down, half-facing her, and said:

"You have been very brave, Yursa, and I thought, although I do not think we should linger on the subject, you would want to know what I have done about what occurred last night."

She looked at him quickly, then away as if she were shy, and he said:

"I visited *Madame* de Salône this morning, and informed her that she must never again set foot on any property that I own, and that if she attempts to hurt you, or anybody else, I would have her taken before the Magistrates. If that happened, she would undoubtedly receive a long prison sentence."

Yursa drew in her breath.

"D-did . . . she believe . . . you?" she asked hesitatingly.

"She believed me!" the *Duc* replied in a hard voice.

"She . . . she must be . . . very angry."

"I think at the same time," the *Duc* said, "she realised that I was not speaking lightly."

He paused before he added:

"You must forgive me, Yursa, for not realising before what she was like. But how could I have imagined, how could I possibly have guessed that she was a Witch?"

There was silence until Yursa said in a very low voice:

"She is . . . evil!"

"I realise that now," the *Duc* agreed. "And I was foolish not to realise before the extent of her wickedness."

His voice changed as he went on:

"It is all over, and what I want you to do is to forget it!"

"I will . . . try to do . . . so."

"Perhaps it would be easier, and in fact you will feel safer," the *Duc* said, "if I were always there to protect you."

He saw by the expression on Yursa's face that she did not understand, and he said very gently:

"I am asking you to marry me, Yursa. I will not only keep you safe, but I feel we would be very happy."

After he had spoken, the *Duc* waited for the radiance he expected to see in Yursa's eyes which he knew would sweep away her paleness and the last traces of what she had suffered.

To his surprise, however, she turned her head and looked away from him out of the window.

She did not speak until he said:

"I asked you to marry me!"

"I . . . I know," Yursa replied without looking at him, "and I am . . . of course very . . . honoured. I know it is what Grandmama wanted, but . . . please . . . I want to . . . g-go home."

"That I understand," the *Duc* said, "but before you leave, shall we tell your grandmother we are engaged?"

Yursa clasped her hands together, and now she looked at him, then away again.

"I . . . I am sorry if it seems . . . rude," she faltered, "and I know how . . . important you are . . . and how much the *Château* and everybody who . . . belongs to it means to . . . Grandmama . . . but I . . . cannot marry . . . you!"

"*Cannot* marry me?" the *Duc* repeated.

What he said sounded stupid even to himself, but he had never imagined for one instant that any woman to whom he offered marriage would refuse him.

For years he had been pursued and pleaded with by his mother and his family to marry again.

It had never struck him for one instant that any woman, whoever she might be, whom he asked to be his wife would turn him down.

"I . . . I am sorry . . . I am . . . very sorry," Yursa said. "I think you are . . . magnificent . . . and I shall always be eternally . . . grateful to you for saving me last night . . . but . . . but I do not want to . . . s-stay here."

"I can understand that because you have been frightened," the *Duc* conceded, "but I have a number of other houses on my estates in which you

108

could stay, and, of course, we will plan a long honey-moon in different parts of the world."

He smiled at her before he said:

"When we come back, I think you will learn to love Montvéal as I do."

There was silence, and he was aware that Yursa was trying to find the words in which to answer him.

He put out his hand as if to take hers, then saw that she was shrinking away from him.

"It is . . . not just . . . the *Château*," Yursa said in a low, hesitating little voice, "or even . . . *Madame* de Salône . . . it is that I . . . do not . . . love you."

"You do not love me?" the *Duc* questioned.

Once again he was surprised.

Women had always loved him, and he had taken their feelings for granted.

Although it seemed absurdly conceited, he had never envisaged that any woman he favoured would ever say quite bluntly that she did not.

Yursa rose to her feet.

"Please . . . do not be angry," she pleaded. "I am very . . . honoured that you should ask me to be your wife . . . it is just that I do not . . . want you to be . . . my husband."

There was an irrepressible little tremor in her voice as she spoke.

Then as the *Duc* sat, just looking at her in con-sternation, she turned and ran from the room before he could prevent her from leaving.

He heard her running down the passage and knew she would go to her own room, or perhaps to her grandmother's.

It was then he told himself that he had been a fool.

How could he have been so foolish as to propose to the girl after what she had been through last night?

It would have made her afraid, if of nothing else, of the *Château*, and what had taken place on the estate.

And yet, he told himself frankly, it was not because of the *Château* that Yursa had refused him, but because of himself.

He saw now that he should have been more perceptive and certainly more intelligent and to have wooed Yursa before he had proposed marriage.

He had known exactly what was intended when Lady Helmsdale had arrived with her granddaughter.

At first it had merely amused him thinking that yet another trap had been set to inveigle him into matrimony.

Yet soon he realised Yursa was different from any of the other women who had been produced as bait to ensnare him.

To begin with, she looked more beautiful than he imagined any young girl could look.

Secondly, he had been aware of her intelligence, and thirdly, he had been surprised, intrigued, and astounded that she could read his thoughts.

Last night, after he had saved her from being burned to death at the stake, he had known she was everything he desired in a wife.

Her innocence, purity, and incredible courage appealed to him in a manner that no other woman had done in the past.

After he had saved her, she had not clung to him in the way he knew only too well was merely another manner of ensuring that his arms encircled the woman in question.

He would then have kissed her, sweeping away any of the discomfort from which she was suffering.

Yursa had cried like a child, weeping in exactly the same manner she would have wept against her father's shoulder, or her mother's.

The *Duc* rose to his feet to stand staring blindly out into the garden.

"I have been a fool," he told himself, "and a conceited one at that!"

He had been so sure that Yursa had come to Montvéal with the same determination to marry him as he knew her grandmother had.

Now, for the first time in his life, he had met a woman who did not want to marry him.

He was aware that he wanted Yursa in a way that was different from any woman he had desired in the past.

Because their thoughts were so closely attuned, he knew she would understand and enjoy helping him look after his estates.

She would also understand his position as head of the family.

He had not missed her politeness and her consideration for the older men and women amongst his guests, and almost everybody had praised her to him.

He knew they were signifying their approval to

what they thought was his inevitable marriage to her.

It had made him determined not to surrender his freedom too quickly, even though from the moment he had met her he had realised that Yursa was exceptional.

He knew now that she was exactly the sort of person he required as his wife.

"But she does not want me as a husband!"

He repeated the words to himself and found them hard to believe.

Every woman, even though they were already married, had always told him he was their ideal.

How often, when the flames of passion had allowed them to speak, had he heard a soft voice say:

"Oh, darling César, if only we could have met before I was married! How different everything would have been!"

He had told himself somewhat cynically that while the woman had aroused in him an irresistible desire, if she had been a *jeune fille*, it was doubtful if he would have noticed her.

And if he had, he was quite certain he would not have proposed marriage.

Now it was something he had done at last, after so many years of prevaricating and fighting off every suggestion from his mother.

Incredibly, he had made a mess of it!

"I will have to start again," he told himself, "I must woo Yursa as I should have done from the very beginning, then I am quite certain she will fall in love with me."

He thought complacently and with some satisfaction of the women who had thrown their hearts at his feet, and loved him overwhelmingly.

Yet inevitably he had become restless and bored.

They had tried to enslave him, to capture him, and it had meant that like a wild animal he had made a frantic bid for freedom.

The more he thought about it, the more he realised that Yursa had never shown the slightest sign of desiring him as a man.

She had listened to him intently, and been thrilled by what he told her about the history of Burgundy and the treasures of Montvéal.

Looking back, he could not remember anything she had said or even one look which would have told him that he fascinated her as a human being.

"How could I have been so obtuse and idiotic?" he asked himself angrily.

For the first time, César de Montvéal looked at himself dispassionately, and was not very impressed by what he saw.

He was a man who possessed everything material that he could possibly desire.

Yet he realised that in the past years, since his wife had become insane, then died, that he had gradually lost much of the spiritual side of his nature.

This he was aware had been predominant during his boyhood, and when he first grew up.

It was not only his faith in God which he liked to believe was unshakable.

He had the ambition to assist, inspire, and lead those who looked up to him because of his position in life.

He thought that he must do good, not because it

was his duty, but because he himself wished to.

But the "primrose path" he had trod so easily had gradually swept away from him everything but his own selfish interest.

He had become preoccupied with a desire to be amused, to succeed in material ways, and the rest had been forgotten.

The *Duc* walked backward and forward across his Study as he criticised himself as he had so often criticised others.

He wished Yursa had not left him, so that he could have told her what he was thinking.

He wondered if he could change her opinion of him and make her feel for him what he felt for her.

"I want her," he said aloud. "I want her as my wife, and, by God, I intend to have her!"

He wondered, if he sent a servant upstairs to ask her to come back to him, whether she would do so.

Then he was afraid of risking a refusal which would be a tit-bit of gossip in the Servants' Hall.

*   *   *

As it happened, Yursa had not gone to her bed-room, as the *Duc* had imagined, but to her grandmother's.

She had knocked lightly on the door, thinking that if the Dowager were asleep she would not hear her.

Then she heard her call out "Come in!" and entered.

Her grandmother was lying on a *chaise longue* in the window with a beautifully embroidered silk cover over her.

"Yursa, dear child!" she exclaimed. "I thought you were with César."

"I was, Grandmama."

Yursa walked across the room to kneel down beside the *chaise longue*, and look up at Lady Helmsdale with an expression which made her ask quickly:

"What is the matter? What has upset you?"

"I . . . I want to . . . go home, Grandmama!"

"Home, dear child? But why? There is no reason for us to leave for at least another week!"

"I want to go . . . back to . . . Papa."

There was silence, then Lady Helmsdale asked:

"Will you give me a reason?"

"I . . . I have just . . . refused the *Duc*'s offer of marriage!"

The words were hesitating, but Lady Helmsdale heard them and stared at her granddaughter in consternation.

"You have refused César?"

"Y-yes . . . Grandmama."

"But, why? Why?"

"Because I do not . . . love him! I am sorry . . . Grandmama, and I know how . . . disappointed you will be, but I have no wish to . . . marry him."

Yursa spoke quietly but firmly as she added:

"I know Papa would not have me . . . forced into a . . . marriage I do not want."

Her grandmother just stared at her, apparently speechless at what she had just heard, then Yursa rose and kissed her on the cheek, saying:

"Forgive me . . . Grandmama, I know you are . . . upset, but there is . . . nothing I can . . . do about . . . it."

She walked across the room towards the door, and

only as she reached it did Lady Helmsdale find her voice.

"Yursa, do not leave! Let us talk about this!"

"There is . . . nothing to talk . . . about," Yursa replied. "But, please . . . arrange for us to . . . leave either . . . to-morrow . . . or the next day."

She did not wait for her grandmother to reply, but went from the room, closing the door behind her.

chapter six

HAVING walked about the Study for some time, the *Duc* then decided, as he could not see Yursa, to go riding.

He went to the stables and chose, instead of one of his new spirited stallions that needed breaking in, a horse he had owned for years.

It nuzzled him affectionately when he patted it.

He knew it was the sort of mount he wanted when he wished to think and not concern himself with mastering a young animal who was fighting him.

He rode away unaware that the grooms looked after him apprehensively.

They had seen the scowl on his face and the expression in his eyes which told them he was perturbed.

Because many of them had known him since he was a boy, they were receptive to every mood, and they wanted above all things for their master to be happy.

The *Duc* rode, first of all, down from the *Château* into the woods, and almost as if he could not help himself, he rode into *le Bois du Dragon*.

He had a feeling that he must see it as it was and convince himself that what had happened there last night was something which would never occur again.

His interview this morning with Zelée was something he did not wish to think about, or remember.

She had greeted him with a self-assurance which to his astonishment was not false.

It was difficult for him to recognise in the smartly dressed soignée woman who came into the room where he was waiting for her, the wild, drugged creature who had tried to murder Yursa.

"*Chèr* César!" she had exclaimed. "How delightful to see you!"

It was then with his eyes hardening and his voice like a whip, the *Duc* had told her what he thought of her and her evil intentions.

She listened to him with a faint smile at the corners of her lips and a disconcerting glint in her eyes.

He had the feeling that he was not hurting her, and she was quite unashamed of her behaviour.

In fact, she might not even remember exactly what had occurred.

He did not allow her to speak but merely informed her forcefully with an undeniable violence that he exiled her from his estate and warned her what he would do if she disobeyed him.

When finally he turned towards the door to leave

she had merely said in a soft, sensuous tone that he knew so well:

"*Au revoir, Mon Brave*, you will miss me as I will miss you, and when you do, all this unpleasantness will be forgotten!"

"Never, as far as I am concerned!" the *Duc* retorted.

He went from the room, slamming the door behind him.

Now, when he reached the clearing in the wood, he thought that the stake in the centre of it, and the half-burnt logs, were the only thing that could convince him that the whole episode had not been just a bad dream.

How could any woman who was supposedly civilised, educated, and accepted in Society be a Witch?

How could she have collected together all those foolish peasant girls, and persuaded them to follow her without there being an uproar in the neighbourhood?

He drew his horse to a standstill and sat looking at the scene which last night had been an expression of an evil he did not know existed.

He knew it had been easy for Zelée, with her brains, to seduce the peasants by the sheer fear of her powers.

Witchcraft had for long existed in certain parts of France, particularly in the sixteenth and seventeenth centuries.

When he thought about it, he had a picture in the *Château* of a Witches' Sabbat which his father had put away in a locked cupboard for fear it should disturb the servants.

He had heard of the Witch Hunts in Scotland and the North of England.

There thousands of innocent women had been branded as Witches and condemned to death after suffering unbelievable tortures.

At the same time, there had been stories of the Black Mass being performed in Paris, and certain sections of the community becoming Satanists.

Yet it was something he had never expected to be perpetrated in Burgundy.

And he could not imagine that he should be associated and, if he were honest, infatuated with a Witch.

Because he could not bear to think of what would have happened if he had not saved Yursa at almost the last minute, he rode away.

He decided that he would have everything cleaned up.

He would also send for the wood-cutters to cut down a number of trees.

The mere fact that they were working there would, he hoped, discourage the Witches, if they persisted in their evil ways, from using that wood again.

He wondered what else he could do to make sure they remained in hiding and did not persuade any other foolish young women into joining them.

He rode on, knowing that he was ashamed of his own lack of intelligence by being ensnared by Zelée, and understanding what Yursa felt about him.

"Of course she would shun a man who had been connected with evil," his common sense told him. "And with her decency and purity, she would believe that anyone who touched pitch would be defiled by it."

But that did not answer his problem.

"What can I do?" he asked.

He rode down to his vineyards and felt they were of little importance beside the love he could feel growing almost every passing moment for Yursa.

He could hardly believe that what he felt was not a figment of his imagination.

And yet he was honest enough to admit it was love and very different from what he had thought was love in the past.

His desire for women had been a flame which ignited between them, had made every glance of their eyes, every movement of their bodies an enticement.

With Yursa it was different.

He knew now that she was a part of the beauty he could see all around him—the rich crops in the valley, the wood-covered hills, and the sunshine overhead.

Because he loved her, she was also to him part of his faith.

It was so ingrained in his soul that even the wiles of Zelée had not prevented it from being there like a light in front of the altar.

"Forgive me, Lord," the *Duc* prayed in his heart.

He knew he must make reparation for the sins he had committed, even if some of them were unknowingly.

At the same time, he was aware that in failing himself and his own ideals, he had failed his family and the ancient blood which pulsated through his veins.

He had also failed Montvéal, which stood for everything in which he believed, and to which he owed his allegiance.

He was a long way from home when finally he turned round, knowing he must go back.

He wondered as he did so if he could approach Yursa again and tell her of his love.

He had done everything where she was concerned in the wrong way.

He had believed that she would have fallen in love with him, as every other woman had done in the past, only to find he was mistaken.

Now he had to make reparation for his own stupidity.

If he was to win Yursa, he had to persuade her that, as he now believed with his whole heart, they were made for each other.

He could see all too clearly, as he had not seen before, that she with her intrinsic purity and perception was the complement of himself.

He was completely convinced that if they were married, he would be able to dedicate his whole life to making her happy.

He saw the *Château* in a different light from the way he had seen it in the past; not just a Museum of treasures, not just a place where he reigned supreme as the *Duc* de Montvéal, but—home.

That was what he had really always wanted; a place where he could be content not as a *Duc*, but as a man.

He wanted to bring up his children in an atmosphere of happiness and contentment which would enable them, when they were old enough, to face the world with confidence and faith in their own ability to succeed.

"How can I explain to Yursa that that is what I want?" he asked.

He knew that was what she wanted, too, but for the moment not with him.

He had ridden so far and covered so much of his own land, that by the time the *Château* came in sight, the sun had lost much of its warmth.

The shadows were growing longer and soon the day would be over.

The *Duc* wondered what Yursa had done during the afternoon, and if she had thought of him as he had been thinking of her.

Because of the way he had left, he approached Montvéal through the wood, climbing up a twisting path which led to the plateau on which it stood.

To reach the front of the *Château* he had to pass the Chapel.

Just as he neared it, a child—a girl of perhaps ten or eleven years of age—came running towards him from the door surmounted by a cross.

The *Duc* wondered who she was and realised as she came nearer that she was pretty, with dark curly hair hanging on each side of her face.

She was wearing a clean but worn dress which was patched in several places.

"*Monsieur, Monsieur!*" she called.

He drew his horse to a standstill as she reached him.

She curtsied as she did so, crying out urgently:

"*Monsieur!* Help! My little brother has fallen into

a deep hole in the Chapel. He's crying, but I cannot reach him!"

"A hole in the Chapel?" the *Duc* repeated.

Then he understood and said:

"I think you mean the Crypt."

"Quickly, *Monsieur*—help him! Please—help him! He is crying and I'm frightened for him!"

The *Duc* dismounted, leaving his horse, who he knew would come when he whistled, free to crop the sparse grass outside the low wall of the court-yard.

Walking across the paving, he hurried into the Chapel.

There was light from in front of the altar and from the candles flickering in the Lady Chapel and in front of the statue of Joan of Arc.

The *Duc* went quickly to the opening of the Crypt, which was not far from the West Door.

As he expected, the iron door which covered it so that it was level with the stone floor of the Chapel was lying open.

He peered down into the darkness, the child beside him saying:

"He was crying, *Monsieur*, and now he's quiet. Perhaps he's dead!"

"No, of course not," the *Duc* said reassuringly. "But he may have hurt himself."

As he spoke he started to climb down the wooden ladder attached to the wall which led into the depths of the Crypt.

He had descended for about eight feet and walked a short distance before the Crypt narrowed and the ceiling became lower.

There was no sign of the little boy.

Then as he moved slowly, looking closely into the darkness, he heard a sharp bang above him.

He realised with surprise that the door of the Crypt had been closed.

"Leave that open," he shouted, "otherwise I cannot see!"

There was no reply, but he heard to his astonishment the sound of the bolt being shot into place.

For a moment he thought he must be mistaken, then in the darkness he heard the sound of water, and although it seemed incredible, he realised he had been trapped.

The Crypt had been used during the Revolution to hide many of the treasures from the *Château*.

They had been placed in strong-boxes, and the Crypt flooded so that enemies or thieves had not thought it worthwhile to search through the deep water.

Now the *Duc* was aware that if somebody, and it was not hard to guess who was behind all this, flooded the Crypt while he was locked inside, he would be drowned.

He stood still, considering his position, and wondering how he could save himself.

There was, he knew, an outlet for the water at the far end of the Crypt.

But he could remember that it was not large enough for him to manipulate himself through it.

In fact, he could recall when he was a small boy trying to climb out of the Crypt that way when one of his friends had locked him in as a joke, and finding it impossible.

"What am I to do?" he asked.

In order to make sure that he was not mistaken in what had happened, he climbed back up the wooden ladder.

When he could reach the iron door he put up his arm to press against it.

He had been right in thinking it had been bolted, and he knew it would be impossible, however hard he tried, to force it open.

It was then he shouted.

"Help! Help me! Help!"

There was no response.

At this time of the evening his Private Chaplain would have finished his Evening Prayers and retired to his apartments, which were some distance away inside the *Château*.

Often there were villagers and Nuns who came to pray, but not this late because of the steep climb to the Chapel through the woods.

It was an even longer distance up the drive on the other side of the *Château*, which was used by carriages.

The *Duc* stood on the ladder, pushing at the door again and again only to know that it would be easier to push down a stone wall than to open the bolted door.

He was aware that beneath him the Crypt was flooding quicker than he had ever known.

He had the idea that whoever had planned his death in this way had tampered with the age-old apparatus.

The water was pouring in, and he reckoned that by now it would be a foot or so deep.

This meant that in a very short while the water

would be up to his shoulders, then over his head.

Desperately, to test if he was right, he climbed down and found that the water nearly reached the top of his riding-boots.

He pulled off his coat, flung it down, and, climbing up the ladder once again, started to push even harder than he had before at the bolted door.

Once again he cried out for help, and as he did so he thought of Yursa.

He remembered how she had read his thoughts.

Now he told himself that his only chance of salvation was if she could hear him calling to her and realise that he was in danger.

"Help me! Save me!" he shouted aloud, and felt as if his whole mind and soul were winging towards her.

"Help me, Yursa! Save me! I do not want to die!"

The words came involuntarily to his lips and he added a prayer.

"God, make her hear me!"

*　　*　　*

Yursa had spent the afternoon when she had left her grandmother in the *Boudoir* which adjoined her bed-room.

She sat there quietly, hardly noticing the fragrance of the flowers, or the beauty of the small room.

Instead, she was longing for the safety and security of England, the house where she had been born and where she had been so happy with her father and mother.

There everything was peaceful and quiet, and she thought once she returned home she would feel safe.

She would be able to forget the horror of last

night, the screams of the Witches, and the evil in
Zelée de Salône's eyes.

She prayed that the evil she had felt emanating
from them when they invoked Satan would be erased
from her mind.

Yet she knew that never again would she read
about or hear of Witches without feeling the fear of
them striking through her like forked lightning.

"I will be safe, Mama, when I am home with
Papa," she whispered.

She felt she could see her mother smile at her,
and she shut her eyes and thought that she was a
child again, saying her prayers at her mother's knee.

A long time later she realised that the afternoon
was drawing to a close and soon it would be time for
her to change for dinner.

She knew she must go down to the Dining-Room
and behave as if nothing had happened.

At the same time, she shrank from seeing the
Duc.

He had asked her to marry him, but how could
she marry a man who had loved a Witch?

She remembered how Zelée de Salône had said
that he belonged to her and she would never let him
go.

Yursa was sure that was true.

Somehow the Witch would gain ascendancy over
him, even though for the moment he repudiated her.

"I want to go home!" Yursa repeated to herself.

She knew she was running away, but there was
nothing else she could do.

Then suddenly she heard the *Duc* calling her.

Because it seemed so real, she stopped thinking and listened.

There was only silence, and she thought she must have dreamt it.

Then she heard him again, and was aware that the voice was in her mind and not in reality.

And yet it was so clear, so strong, that it was as if it were speaking in the very depths of her heart.

"I am imagining things!" she told herself.

Yet she knew his thoughts were reaching out to her, and she heard them just as she had when they were together.

"If he wants me, I will not go to him," she told herself defiantly.

Suddenly she heard him quite clearly saying:

"Yursa, save me! For God's sake, save me!"

He was in danger, but why? And how could she be sure of it?

Inevitably she thought of Zelée de Salône.

Could she be now harming the *Duc* as she had tried to harm her?

She was evil, and Yursa could feel the vibrations of evil emanating once again from her.

It was so strong that she knew she must go to the Chapel, for only in the Chapel was she near to God.

The living Sacrament which was enshrined there would combat the evil of a Witch.

She opened the door of her *Boudoir,* and as she did so, she could hear the *Duc* calling her even more urgently than he had before.

"Save me—oh—Yursa—save me!"

It was then, without really considering it, she began to run.

He needed her, and because it seemed to be somehow concerned with *Madame* de Salône, she must reach the sanctuary of the Chapel.

She sped along the corridor and down the stairs, reaching the door which opened into the court-yard.

There she hesitated for a moment, then, seeing the Chapel door was open, she ran to it.

It was then, as she did so, her eyes on the flickering light in front of the Altar, that she heard again the *Duc's* voice.

It was not now in her mind, but somewhere beneath her feet.

"Help me! Help me—Yursa! Save—me!"

She turned bewildered in the direction from which the sound had come and realised it was underneath the ground.

"I am here! Where are you?" she called, and thought as she spoke that this must be part of her imagination.

Then she heard his voice.

"The door of the Crypt—it is bolted! Open it—quickly!"

It was difficult to see, but Yursa thought later that it was just instinct which made her see the trap-door in the ground and the bolt which lay across it.

She pulled at it with all her strength and, strangely enough, as if it had just been oiled, it slid back.

As it did so, the door was pushed open and she saw first the *Duc's* hand and arm appear.

Then his head emerged from the darkness of the water which covered him up to his neck.

She gave a little cry at the sight of him, and as he

clambered up, the water swishing onto the floor, she exclaimed:

"She was . . . trying to . . . drown you! But . . . you are . . . safe! Safe!"

The *Duc* stepped onto the stone floor, saying as he did so:

"I am safe, my darling, thanks to you, although, God knows, if you had come a few minutes later, it would have been too late!"

"But you are . . . all right," Yursa breathed.

Then she was not certain how it happened, but she put out her arms, he pulled her against him, and his lips came down on hers.

For a moment she was too surprised to realise what was happening.

Then as he held her closer and his lips took possession of her she knew that she loved him.

She knew, too, that if he had been drowned, she would have lost everything in life that mattered.

He kissed her at first violently with the sheer relief that he was alive.

Then, as he felt the softness and innocence of her lips, his kiss became more gentle, more tender.

He pulled her closer and closer still, and although, because his shirt was wet, the water soaked through her gown, Yursa was not aware of it.

She knew only that her whole being was surging with an inexpressible rapture because the *Duc* was alive, when he might have died.

She had saved him from the Witch, and she loved him.

He kissed her and went on kissing her and she felt

as if she gave him not only her heart, but her mind, her soul, her body.

She was a part of him and there was nothing else in the world but him.

Then he raised his head and said in a voice that was curiously unsteady:

"I am making you wet, my precious!"

"You are . . . alive . . . and I . . . love you!"

"That is what I want to hear."

He was kissing her again; kissing her with long, slow, passionate kisses which made her feel as if he swept her into the sky and her feet were no longer upon earth.

At last, as if he came back from the Heavens where she had taken him, the *Duc* said:

"How could you be so wonderful as to have heard me? I knew that only you would be aware that I was in danger and my life hung by a thread."

"I heard you . . . I heard . . . you! And I knew . . . that because you were . . . menaced by . . . evil I must . . . go to the . . . Chapel."

"I have never been so near to death before!"

"But . . . you are . . . alive!" she whispered.

She put her cheek, as she spoke, against his shoulder and realised how wet he was.

"You must take off these wet clothes," she said, "or you will catch . . . a chill."

The *Duc* laughed.

"A chill will not matter as long as I can live, breathe, and tell you I love you."

He would have pulled her close to him again, but he said:

"We will go back to the *Château*, but first I must turn off the water."

As he spoke he looked down and realised that the water was overflowing and they were standing in a puddle which was spreading over the stone floor.

Yursa quickly moved her feet away from it and the *Duc* looked at the side of the wall.

There was a small wheel which could turn on the water in the Crypt, but when he looked for it, he realised the wheel had been removed.

The water would therefore pour through without being able to be checked.

He knew, although he did not say so to Yursa, that it was on Zelée's orders that it had been tampered with.

Now nobody could have saved him by preventing the Crypt from overflowing.

He thought he would send somebody from the *Château* to attend to it, and went back to Yursa.

They had opened the door and now in the evening light he could see how wet he had made her pretty gown.

Her face, too, was wet from his kisses, but the only thing that mattered was that her eyes were looking into his, and they radiated the love he had longed to see there.

"I love you," he said in his deep voice, "and when I am looking more respectable than I am at the moment, I will tell you how much!"

"All that . . . matters is that . . . you are . . . alive," Yursa whispered.

The way she spoke was very moving.

They were standing in the open door of the

Chapel, and now she turned to look towards the Altar.

"Shall we come back . . . later and thank God that He sent . . . me to . . . you in . . . time?"

"We will do that," the *Duc* replied quietly.

They both genuflected, then hand in hand went across the court-yard towards the *Château*.

The *Duc* remembered as he went that he must send a groom to collect his horse, as well as a man to attend to the water.

* * *

Below the East window of the Chapel was a sluice-gate through which the water from the Crypt could run out.

As Zelée de Salône arrived there, climbing up the side of the hill through the trees to it, she found as she had ordered that the shrubs and ivy which covered the gate had been cleared away.

On her instructions there was nobody there, and it was late in the evening.

She thought with satisfaction that in a short while the body of the *Duc* drowned in the Crypt would come through the sluice-gate and she would carry it away.

She had it all planned in her mind that he would vanish and nobody would know what had happened to him.

She would be able to laugh as the noble family searched for him in vain.

What she did not know was that the sluice-gate, while it looked large enough to allow a man to come through it, was inside too small for him to do so.

She had watched through the trees, and listened to the *Duc* going to the Chapel in answer to the child's plea for help.

She calculated exactly how long it would take to fill the Crypt with water, and the *Duc* to be drowned.

Because the sluice-gate was old, there was now a trickle coming from between the two doors which closed in the centre.

She watched it with glowing eyes, telling herself it was like the *Duc's* blood which she had shed because he had refused her and tried to exile her from his land.

Now, she told herself, he would lie in an unmarked grave, and not in the vaults of his ancestors.

"Then he will be mine! Mine, for ever!"

She told herself she had been clever to strike so quickly before anybody was aware that he had denounced her for her perfidy.

"I will dedicate his body to Satan, who will take his soul," she told herself with glee.

Then she was aware that the trickle of water had ceased and she mused in perplexity.

By now the Crypt shoud be full, and the *Duc* drowned.

Then it suddenly struck her that was what had happened, and his body would block the channel to prevent the water from escaping.

She climbed down to the sluice-gate, which was a little lower than the rock on which she had been standing.

To open the trap-door she had to use all her

strength to raise the catch that was a strong and substantial one.

She used both her hands, then, because it was well-oiled, the catch moved back and the doors opened.

Then Zelée saw that what she had thought was the *Duc* was in fact his coat, which had prevented the water from dripping as it had been doing.

Even as she put out her hand towards it, the water burst like an explosion through the pipe straight into her chest.

It knocked her off her feet with a violence that swept her along the stony path which lay just in front of the sluice-gate.

It carried her to where there was a fall of rock.

Zelée screamed as like a flood-tide it threw her over the edge.

She fell, still screaming onto the rocks about thirty feet lower down.

The water poured over her; but she was still, her neck broken in the fall.

*　　*　　*

A peasant coming back from the fields saw her lying amongst the rocks.

He thought her skirt was a piece of material which might be useful to his wife.

When he went to pick it up he saw it was a woman, lying face downwards.

When he turned the body over he could see that her face, smashed in by her fall, was distorted and disfigured.

He realised there was nothing he could do and that the woman was dead.

Because he told himself it was not his business, and he had no wish to be involved in what looked like an unpleasant accident or murder, he walked quickly away.

As he did so, he crossed himself and said a prayer to the Saints that he would not be involved in anything unpleasant.

Nor, for that matter, would he have to explain why he was in the wood instead of going home through the fields.

Earlier in the day he had set two rabbit-snares under the trees which led into *le Bois du Dragon*, where he knew nobody was likely to go late at night.

He decided to collect them quickly in case anybody nosing about trying to find the dead woman should be inquisitive enough to discover them instead.

In one of them there was a fat young rabbit which he knew would make him a good supper.

He slipped it into his capacious pocket and hurried on.

He told himself that in future, he would snare his supper in another part of the woods, where a dead body was not likely to be lying about.

chapter seven

WHEN Yursa reached her bed-room she realised that
the front of her gown was very wet.

She took it off quickly and hid it so that when
Jeanne appeared, she would not have to answer any
questions.

She knew without discussing it that the *Duc*
would not wish anybody in the *Château* to realise
how *Madame* de Salône had tried to drown him.

He had been within a few seconds of death.

She felt herself shiver at the thought, and although it was wonderful to know that the *Duc* was
alive, she was still afraid.

She was quite certain that Zelée de Salône would
not cease her Witchcraft.

Having failed to burn her at the stake, and drown
the *Duc*, she would think up some other and more
frightening way in which to dispose of both of them.

For a moment Yursa felt a panic of fear sweep over her, then she knew that God, having saved them both from destruction, would save them again.

Good must triumph over evil.

She felt as if her mother were telling her so, and there was no reason for her to be afraid.

She wiped herself down, then, putting on a night-gown, slipped into bed to lie down.

There was still time for her to have a rest.

She knew if she were to look attractive for the *Duc* that night, and she wanted that above all else, she would be wise to try to sleep.

She shut her eyes and felt his arms around her, his lips on hers.

She felt within herself the rising ecstasy he had given her and knew it was a rapture beyond anything she had ever imagined.

"I love . . . him! I love him!" she said in her heart.

She vowed she would try to protect him in every way she could for the rest of her life.

She realised that one of the reasons that her feelings for the *Duc* had changed so quickly was he had needed her.

When he emerged from the water in the Crypt, she thought of him not as the grand *Duc* whom her grandmother wished her to marry, but as a man whom she could protect and comfort.

She knew she would feel the same way if she had a son.

She wanted to give the *Duc* children who would fill Montvéal with love and who would be as hand-some as he was.

Then like a cold hand squeezing her heart she

thought that if they had children, they, too, might be menaced by Zelée de Salône and her evil.

Once again she was praying—praying with all her heart to God to help her and the man she loved.

She must have dozed for a little while, for she awoke to hear the door open softly and Jeanne come into the room.

She smiled at the maid and asked:

"Is it time for me to dress for dinner?"

"There is no hurry, *M'mselle*," Jeanne replied. "I have a message from *Monsieur le Duc* to say that he is taking you out to dinner, and there is no reason for you to come downstairs until eight o'clock."

"Out to dinner?" Yursa exclaimed in astonishment.

Then she realised that the *Duc* thought that it would be embarrassing for them, feeling as they did, to be with other people.

'He is taking me somewhere where we can be alone,' she thought, and felt her heart leap.

She was shy of her love and she knew she could not bear to have what remained of the *Duc*'s guests looking at her curiously, and perhaps asking questions.

"He is so wonderful," she told herself. "He thinks of everything."

She lay back with closed eyes thinking of him while Jeanne tidied the room and prepared her bath.

Only when it was ready, the warm water scented with the fragrance of syringa, did she get out of bed.

The bath soaked away any tiredness she felt; yet she did not want to linger in it because she longed to be with the *Duc*.

She realised that when she did go downstairs his

guests would all be in the Dining-Room, and there would be nobody to see them leave the *Château*.

She felt, too, he would have made some explanation to her grandmother.

There was no need to think of anything but of making herself look attractive for him.

She was so intent on thinking of the *Duc*'s kisses that only when she was dressed did she realise that she was wearing the prettiest gown her grandmother had brought her from Paris.

It was one she would have chosen for this night of all nights if Jeanne had not somehow guessed it was what she should wear.

Designed by Worth, it was a combination of chiffon, gauze, and tulle, the frills of the bustle ornamented with an exquisite shadow lace which also encircled the bodice.

The way it was cut made her waist look tiny.

She hoped when she looked in the mirror that the *Duc* would think she resembled some of his precious orchids.

Because she was going out, Jeanne gave her lace mittens which were so fine that they might have been woven by spiders.

There was a wrap of white velvet trimmed with swansdown to put round her shoulders.

"You look very, very lovely, *M'mselle!*" Jeanne said.

Yursa thanked her before leaving and going slowly down the stairs.

The *Duc* was waiting for her in the hall.

There was nobody else except for two footmen to see them go hand in hand down the red carpet and into the closed carriage that was waiting at the bottom of the steps.

Only as they drove off did Yursa say:

"How could you have thought of anything so... wonderful as our being... alone this... evening?"

"I thought it would please you," the *Duc* said.

He took her hand in his, pulled off the mitten, and kissed her fingers, one by one.

Then he turned her hand over and kissed the palm, and she quivered with sensations she had never known before.

"I love you," he said, "and I grudge every minute you are away from me!"

"I have been... thinking of... you."

"And praying for me?"

"Praying that I can look... after and... protect you," she replied with a little tremor in her voice.

"That is what I have been doing too," he said, "and, darling, we must have faith and believe that now that we are together, our love will defend us against all evil."

Yursa's fingers tightened on his.

"I want to be... sure of... that," she said, "but you must... help me."

He put his arm around her, but he did not kiss her, and they drove in silence. There was no need for words.

Only as in a very short time they turned off the road through some wrought-iron gates did she ask:

"Where are we going?"

"We are dining at my mother's *Château*," the *Duc* replied, "because there we can be alone. But I thought you would not mind if we saw my mother first."

"No . . . of course not," Yursa agreed.

The *Duc* did not say any more.

When they stepped out of the carriage, Yursa knew why he had brought her to the beautiful *Château* where his mother lived.

She would not have to think of the Chapel where he had nearly drowned, or the Witch who had been his guest.

She knew without being told that the *Duchesse* would never have entertained *Madame* de Salône, and for to-night, therefore, they were free of her.

She left her velvet wrap in the hall and they went up the stairs to the *Duchesse's* room.

She was not in bed, but sitting in a chair in her *Boudoir* wearing an elegant negligée with wide sleeves.

There were several rows of pearls around her neck and diamonds on her fingers.

The *Duchesse* gave a little cry of gladness when they were announced, and the *Duc*, bending to kiss his mother, said:

"You should not have waited up for us, Mama!"

"I was so pleased when I received your note, my dearest," the *Duchesse* replied, "and Chef has been working frantically to prepare a dinner which I hope will delight you both!"

She held up her hand to Yursa, saying:

"You look very lovely, dear child!"

Then she looked at them and asked a little hesitatingly:

"As you are . . . both here, have you . . . something to . . . tell me?"

Yursa knew from the way the *Duchesse* spoke that she was half-afraid that she was being too optimistic in what she hoped.

"We have come to tell you, Mama," the *Duc* replied, "that Yursa and I love each other."

The *Duchesse* gave a little cry of sheer joy.

"Oh, my darling, is this true?" she asked. "Then God has answered my prayers!"

There were tears in her eyes as she put out one hand to her son and one to Yursa.

They both bent down on one knee beside her chair.

"We are not only in love," the *Duc* said quietly, "but we are going to be married, Mama, here to-night, in your Private Chapel!"

If the *Duchesse* gasped, so did Yursa, and as he spoke he turned to look at her.

She understood without words because she could read his thoughts that if they were married they would be together and very much safer.

Yursa's eyes met his and the *Duc* saw the radiance in her face. Then he said gently:

"You must not cry, Mama, we want you to be as happy as we are."

"I am crying for sheer happiness!" the *Duchesse* replied. "The minute I saw Yursa, I knew she was exactly the right wife for you, and the daughter-in-law I have always wanted."

"You were right, Mama," the *Duc* said, "and I know you will understand that when we are married,

we want to stay here, so that we can be completely
alone."

* * *

A little while later they went downstairs to the Dining-Room.

Yursa found that the *Duc* had ordered that the
servants should leave the room between the courses
when they had served them.

"How could you have planned anything so
quickly?" she asked.

"I knew when you told me you loved me," he answered, "that you not only belonged to me, but that I
wanted you with me by day and by night."

He smiled at her very tenderly before he added:

"It would be agonising to be separated, or to have
to spend precious moments with other people, when
we might be alone."

He saw from the expression in her eyes that that
was what she thought, too, and went on:

"I knew you would not wish after what has just
happened to be married in my Chapel, so I gave my
Chaplain instructions to come here. He will be waiting for us when we are ready."

"I . . . I thought . . ." Yursa began to say

"I know that you are thinking," the *Duc* inter-
rupted, "that in France we have to be married legally
in front of the Mayor, but that has already taken
place by proxy."

She looked at him in surprise as he added:

"You have been, according to the laws of France,
my wife for nearly an hour!"

Yursa laughed.

"Now you are frightening me," she said. "How can you get everything done so quickly so that I am breathless?"

"I want you," he said quietly, "and now you are mine! But I know we both want the blessings of God for our marriage, which must be perfect for the rest of our lives."

Because she was so happy, Yursa could never remember what she had eaten at dinner.

But because she knew it would please the Chef, when they had finished she asked the Butler to thank him and to say it was the most delicious meal she had ever eaten.

The *Duc* said the same, and they left the Dining-Room together.

When they were outside she looked at him enquiringly, wondering what was to happen next.

"If you will go to your room, my precious," he said, "you will find Jeanne waiting for you, and I will come to collect you."

He took her, as he spoke, up the stairs, opened a door, and when Yursa entered she saw Jeanne waiting for her.

It was a very lovely room with a painted ceiling, and a huge bed carved with posts encircled by flowers and supported by gold angels.

There were vases of white lilies that scented the room with their fragrance, but Yursa was looking at Jeanne, who said:

"This, *M'mselle,* is the happiest day of my life!"

"As it is mine, Jeanne!" Yursa replied.

"How could I have guessed—how could I have known, *M'mselle,* when you told me to pack because you were going back to England, that you would marry *Monseigneur?*"

"We are very happy."

She suddenly realised the reason why the *Duc* had brought her to her bed-room for, lying on the bed, was a lace veil as fine as the lace on her gown.

Jeanne told her that all the brides of the Montvéal family had used it at their weddings.

"*Madame la Duchesse* also sent these for you to choose which you prefer," Jeanne added.

She opened two boxes as she spoke.

In one was a tiara of diamonds which encircled the head, and which was very magnificent.

In the other was a wreath of diamond flowers made by one of the great Jewellers in Paris, whom Yursa had heard was a genius at creating flowers.

Jeanne took the wreath from its box, and when Yursa put it on her head she thought it was the most beautiful piece of jewellery she had ever imagined.

Because she wanted to see the *Duc* without there being anything between them, she did not cover her face with the veil.

She told Jeanne to arrange it so that it fell on either side of her face.

Only when she looked in the mirror did she wonder if the *Duc* would have preferred it the other way.

A moment later when he knocked at the door and then came in she saw by the expression in his eyes that she looked exactly the bride he wanted.

She realised then why he had left her, for his evening-coat was now covered with decorations and one—a jewelled cross—hung round his neck onto his shirt-front.

He held in his hand a small bouquet of star-shaped orchids, and when Yursa took them from him their fingers touched and she felt a thrill run through her body like the warmth of sunshine.

When the *Duc* offered her his arm, she put her hand on it and they walked from the bed-room down the stairs and along the corridor.

The Chapel belonging to the *Château* was much smaller than the one at Montvéal.

It had been built in the eighteenth century, and was very beautiful.

It was, however, difficult to see much of it because there were lighted candles on the altar, before every Saint, and along the window-sills beneath the stained-glass windows.

It was a paean of light, and Yursa knew that the *Duc* had ordered it as a thanksgiving because they were both alive and together.

His Chaplain was waiting for them and the only other people present were two Servers wearing red cassocks and lace-edged surplices.

The *Duc* and Yursa knelt to receive the Sacrament.

As they did so she felt as if she could hear the voices of angels and hear the flutter of their wings in the arched roof above them.

It was so real that when the Priest gave them the blessing, Yursa was sure that, as the *Duc* had said, God was protecting them.

Good had triumphed over evil, and they were safe—safe for ever.

When the Service was over, they walked back the way they had come.

Now, when they reached the hall, Yursa was aware that everything was quiet and there were no servants to be seen.

She was therefore not surprised when they entered her bed-room to find that Jeanne was not there either, and she was alone with her husband.

The only light came from a candelabrum by the bed, and as the *Duc* came towards her he thought his wife's eyes were shining like stars.

"I love you, my darling," he said, "and now you are mine!"

Yursa lifted her face to his and thought he would kiss her, but instead he lifted the diamond wreath from her head and put it with her veil on a chair.

Very slowly, as if he savoured the moment, he put his arms around her, and held her very close to him.

"Is this...true...really true?" Yursa asked. "Or am I...dreaming?"

"If it is a dream, then we are dreaming together," the *Duc* said softly.

Then he was kissing her gently and reverently, as if the solemnity of the Marriage Service were still with him.

Only when she tried to move a little closer to him did he say:

"Let me take off my coat, I am afraid my decorations might hurt you."

"I am very proud of them," Yursa said, "and sometime you must tell me what they all mean."

"They mean," he answered, "that I have done a few good things in my life for which I have been rewarded, and now, because I know it will please you, I hope to do a great many more."

"That is what I wanted you to say."

He kissed her and now his lips were more passionate.

He felt her stir and knew her heart was beating as wildly as his as he undid the back of her gown.

She gave a little murmur as it fell to the ground.

Then, moving quickly closer to him, she hid her face in his shoulder.

"Are you shy, my darling?" the *Duc* asked.

"Shy . . . and a little . . . afraid," Yursa whispered.

"Of me?"

"No . . . not of you . . . but in case you are . . . disappointed."

He made a sound that was almost a laugh.

Then he picked her up and carried her in his arms to lay her gently down on the bed with her head on the pillows, and pulled the sheet over her.

She felt she had walked into an enchanted dream.

After having been so depressed and miserable during the afternoon, it was impossible to believe that what she was feeling now could be true.

She felt the sunshine that was always part of the *Duc's* kisses rippling through her like a golden stream.

Then as he lay beside her she turned to once again hide her face against him.

"Everything has been done in such a hurry," the *Duc* said, "and I have therefore had no time to tell you, my beautiful, adorable little wife, how much I love you!"

"I love you . . . too!" Yursa said. "But . . . because I

151

am so...ignorant about love...I am afraid...I might do something...wrong."

"That is impossible, because you are perfect," the *Duc* said. "You are everything I have always sought for, always longed for and thought it impossible to find."

"Is that...true?"

He knew as she spoke she was remembering the many women there had been in his life, and most of all, Zelée.

His lips were on her forehead as he said:

"I must explain to you, my lovely wife, that although I have known many women, I have never, and this is true, felt for any of them what I feel for you!"

"How can I be...different?"

The *Duc* sought for words to explain the difference. Then he said:

"You are too young to understand that a man can be attracted by a woman just because she has a beautiful body."

He felt a little tremor go through Yursa, and knew she was jealous as he went on:

"What a man feels for her and she feels for him is an entirely physical desire which dies away as quickly as it is kindled."

He knew that Yursa was listening and he continued:

"What has happened to me is that although a woman attracted me because I am a man, I find her brain so banal, and her thoughts so commonplace that I have become bored with her whenever we are not making love."

"But . . . she attracted . . . you!" Yursa said.

"Just by her body, and often there has been nothing else," the *Duc* answered.

Then he drew Yursa a little closer and said:

"We are so closely attuned to each other. How else could you have heard me calling to you to save me, or be aware of where I was?"

"It does seem . . . extraordinary."

"That is because our minds are as one," the *Duc* said. "And when I knew I was in love with you, my darling, my heart went out to you, and I think when I kissed your lips you gave me yours."

"It was . . . so wonderful and so . . . exciting," Yursa murmured, "that I thought . . . you had . . . carried me up to . . . Heaven!"

"That is what I want to do again and again," the *Duc* said, "and as I have already told you, it is something I have never felt with anybody else except you."

Yursa moved to look up at him, and he added:

"But there is something else."

"What . . . is that?"

"When we knelt just now in the Chapel," the *Duc* said, "I knew that you felt, as I did, that we received the blessing of God. We were united by our love so that just as no man will ever mean anything to you, no other woman can ever mean anything to me."

Yursa gave a little cry of delight.

"Is that . . . true . . . really . . . true?"

"You know I could not say it at this moment unless it were true!" the *Duc* said in his deep voice. "And if I did lie, you would be aware of it."

"How can we be so lucky . . . so incredibly . . .

wonderfully lucky," Yursa said, "to have . . . found each other?"

The *Duc* did not answer, and she went on:

"I am so foolish that I was . . . afraid of staying with you and I had already had my trunks packed . . . so that I could . . . leave to-morrow."

"Do you really think I would have let you go?" the *Duc* asked. "I knew when I went riding to-day that however long it might take me, I would woo you, pursue you, and hold you prisoner, if necessary, until you loved me!"

"That is exactly what you . . . have done, and very quickly," Yursa said. "I thought I had lost you . . . and when you came out of the Crypt and put your arms around me . . . I knew I had to . . . hold you . . . protect you . . . and save you for the . . . rest of our lives."

As she spoke she felt a little tremor of fear in case their lives would not last very long, and the *Duc* said:

"Forget everything except that we are under the protection of God, and together."

Then he was kissing her; kissing her until she felt once again he had taken her up into Heaven.

He kissed her eyes, her cheeks, the softness of her neck, so that she felt as if the sunshine in her body were turning to flames and flickering through her.

She was aware that there was fire on the *Duc*'s lips as he kissed her lips until she was breathless, then he kissed her breasts.

She wanted him to go on kissing her, and for her to be even closer to him than she was at the moment.

She did not understand what she was feeling, but the *Duc* did, and he knew that never in his whole life had he been so happy or so excited.

At the same time, he was experienced enough to know that he must be very gentle with Yursa so as not to frighten or shock her.

Also that the spiritual side of their love must never be lost in the physical.

But because Yursa loved him with all her heart and soul, everything he did seemed part of the Divine.

When finally he made her his, she knew that the gates of Heaven were open.

* * *

Yursa awoke to realise that what had aroused her was the sound of the curtains being drawn back.

It was still dark outside.

Then, as she wondered why she was seeing a few far-away stars twinkling overhead, the *Duc* came back to bed and took her in his arms.

She moved against him, feeling his strong, athletic body against hers, and because she could not help it, kissing his shoulder to show that she loved him.

Then because she was curious she asked:

"Why have you drawn back the curtains?"

"I thought we would see the dawn together," the *Duc* said, "the dawn of a new day, my darling—the beginning for us both of a new life."

"Do you . . . still love . . . me?"

"How can you ask anything so absurd?" he replied. "I adore you!"

"And . . . you were not . . . disappointed in me?"

"No woman could have been more perfect or more utterly and completely captivating. If I loved you last night, I love you a million times more to-day, and I am sure that will double and increase to-morrow!"

Yursa laughed.

"That is what I was going to say to you, and yester-day morning, when I woke up, I would not even admit that I loved you!"

"And what do you feel now?"

"I adore and . . . worship you," she said a little shyly.

"That is what I want you to say. At the same time, you have to help me and inspire me to be very much better than I am at the moment."

"I want you just as you are," Yursa said, "and I am so happy that I feel as if you have put the stars that . . . have vanished from the sky . . . into my . . . heart."

"That is what I intend to do," the *Duc* said, "and if I can give you the moon and the sun, that would not be enough to express my love."

She put out her hand and drew him a little closer to her.

"You must be very . . . very . . . careful," she said, "because if I should lose you . . . I would want to . . . die."

It flashed through both their minds how near they had been to death, and the *Duc* said:

"We have to live. There is so much for us to do, and I think France needs us, or will need us in the future."

Yursa thought that was how the *Ducs* of Burgundy had felt in the past.

She was sure that the *Duc's* powers would in-crease through the years, and if troubles and difficul-ties came to his country, he would be a leader to whom the people would turn for help.

He was the man she had dreamt about in her dreams, the hero whom she had always been afraid did not exist.

"I love you... I love you!" she said. "How can... you be so... wonderful?"

"I want you to believe that of me," the *Duc* said, "then perhaps it is what I will become."

He thought as he spoke that it would be definitely something he would try to achieve so that his wife and his children would be proud of him.

Then, he thought, when he did come to die, he would not have lived in vain.

Because Yursa was so soft and sweet, and everything he had always longed to find in a woman only to be disappointed, he could only kiss her.

He felt her respond to his kisses as she had done before, with her heart and her soul.

He knew, too, as her body quivered against his, that he had awoken in her the first stirrings of desire, the first need of a woman for a man.

He felt the softness of her skin and the exquisite curves of her breasts and knew that it would be impossible for him to have anything more adorable in his arms.

His love was greater than the fire rising in him and which he knew he was again igniting within Yursa.

It was a love that seemed to come from the Power that poured through them both, and the vibrations which were the Life Force, and which came from their souls.

They had dedicated themselves to the same God

who had protected them against the damnation of evil.

It was something he did not want Yursa to think of, but he felt in himself an overwhelming gratitude.

It was a debt which he must repay throughout his whole life.

Now, because he could feel Yursa quivering against him, and because he could feel the blood throbbing in his temples and his heart beating frantically, it was impossible to think of anything but her and his love.

He kissed her until he knew that she was burning with a need of him as he burned for her.

"I love you, my darling, my precious, beloved little wife," he said, "and I want you, I want you desperately, now, at this moment!"

"I love you, César," Yursa whispered. "Love me ... please ... love me!"

It was a cry that no man could refuse.

As the *Duc* made Yursa his, they both felt as if they were swept by an irresistible force into their own perfect Heaven.

Outside, the dawn broke, the first rays of the sun swept away the darkness, and it was light.

* * *

Jeanne was in the kitchen of the *Château* when one of the grooms arrived from Montvéal.

He had ridden over to deliver a note from the *Duc*'s secretary.

He saw Jeanne and as they greeted each other she said:

"You're early this morning, Gustave!"

"I was told to bring this note for *Monsieur le Duc*," the groom replied.

"Has anything happened at Montvéal?" Jeanne asked.

Gustave glanced over his shoulder to see that none of the other servants were listening.

"I happen to know what's in it," he said confidentially.

"That doesn't surprise me," Jeanne remarked tartly. "There's not much goes on up at the *Château* that you don't know about!"

"That's true enough," Gustave replied with satisfaction, "but this is something special, this is!"

"What is it?"

Because he could not bear to keep the news to himself, Gustave said in a low voice:

"That *Madame* de Salône is dead!"

Jeanne stared at him in utter disbelief.

"I don't believe it!"

"It's true enough. The wood-cutters found her body first thing this morning when they were going to work."

"She was in the wood?" Jeanne enquired.

"At the bottom of the rocks below the Chapel."

"Are you telling me the truth?"

"Cross my heart! Battered she was—and wet! As if water had run all over her!"

"It sounds peculiar to me!" Jeanne said.

"That's what them wood-cutters thought! Afraid, they were, to touch her, knowing what they'd heard about her and her wicked ways!"

Jeanne was silent. Then she asked:

"You say she's dead?"

"Dead as a door-nail!" Gustave replied. "And they've taken her back to her home in a farm-cart."

It struck Jeanne that it was poetic justice that *Madame* de Salône should be carried in a rough cart, because that was what she had used to kidnap *M'mselle* Yursa.

She suddenly realised what a relief the news would be to the *Duc* and his new *Duchesse*.

It would sweep away the last cloud over their happiness.

It was almost as if it had come as a special wedding present before anybody else was aware that they had been married.

She knew, too, that it would please the old *Duchesse*, who had always disliked and mistrusted *Madame* de Salône, as well she might.

"Well, you've brought good news, *Monsieur* Gustave," Jeanne said, "so I'll give you some to take back to the *Château*."

"And what might that be?"

"It is," Jeanne said, speaking slowly and making her words more impressive, "that *Monsieur le Duc* and *M'mselle* Yursa were married last night, here in the Chapel!"

Gustave stared at her in astonishment. Then he said:

"That's very good news, although it's a bit of a surprise!"

Jeanne, who had a good idea why the *Duc* had married in such haste, did not speak, and he went on:

"It's what everybody's been wanting for a long

time, and now there'll be a deal of excitement when I tells them what's occurred."

The satisfaction in Gustave's voice was unmistakable, and Jeanne, taking the note from him, said:

"You can ride back now and tell them up at Mont-véal what's happened."

Gustave hesitated, and she said:

"If you hurry, you'll have time to be back here again before they ring for their breakfast. You've been married yourself, so you know there's no need to hurry on the first morning of your honeymoon!"

Gustave laughed.

Then as he saw the point of what Jeanne was saying, he said:

"You're right, *M'mselle*, I'll ride back, give them the good news, and be back here before you can count the minutes I've been away!"

"You flatter yourself if you think that's what I'm going to do!" Jeanne answered.

She would have turned away with the note in her hand if Gustave had not caught hold of her.

"Give us a kiss to celebrate all the excitement there's going to be when it's known that *Monsieur*'s been caught at last?"

"Get away with you!" Jeanne said pushing him off. "You've got a wife and three children, so keep your kisses to yourself!"

"You don't know what you're missing!" Gustave laughed.

"I've a good idea!" Jeanne replied.

She waited until Gustave had mounted his horse, then went upstairs.

She knew better than anybody else what the information she held in her hand would mean to the *Duc* and *Duchesse*.

She was woman enough to understand Yursa's fear that somehow, in some crafty, evil way, *Madame* de Salône would either entice the *Duc* back into her clutches, or destroy her, as she had tried to do and failed.

"Now they're free to be happy," Jeanne said to herself.

She reached the bed-room door, but there was no sound.

With a smile on her lips, she went and sat down on a chair a little way down the corridor to wait for the bell to ring.

* * *

Inside the room Yursa said:

"I suppose, darling, we should ring for breakfast."

"I am too happy to eat," the *Duc* replied. "I want to stay here all day making love to you and telling you how lucky I am!"

"I should like that, too, but I am afraid you might be bored."

"How could I ever be bored with you?" he asked. "My precious, there are no words to tell you how much I love you, or how beautiful you are."

Yursa put her arm round his neck and drew him a little closer.

The sun was casting a golden light over the whole room and the *Duc*, seeing it glint on her hair, thought she was like the sun itself.

"I love you!" he said. "Why are there no more

162

words in our vocabulary in which to express our love?"

"It is easier to say it in kisses," Yursa said, and lifted her lips to his.

He looked down at her for a long moment, then he said:

"You are right! There is no need for words!"

Then he was kissing her, the sun touched them both, the warmth of it moving from their lips into their hearts.

They were ONE.

ABOUT THE AUTHOR

Barbara Cartland, the world's most famous romantic novelist, who is also an historian, playwright, lecturer, political speaker and television personality, has now written over 470 books and sold nearly 500 million copies all over the world.

She has also had many historical works published and has written four autobiographies as well as the biographies of her mother and that of her brother, Ronald Cartland, who was the first Member of Parliament to be killed in the last war. This book has a preface by Sir Winston Churchill and has just been republished with an introduction by the late Sir Arthur Bryant.

Love at the Helm, a novel written with the help and inspiration of the late Earl Mountbatten of Burma, Great

Uncle of His Royal Highness The Prince of Wales, is being sold for the Mountbatten Memorial Trust.

She has broken the world record for the last twelve years by writing an average of twenty-three books a year. In the Guiness Book of Records she is listed as the world's top-selling author.

Miss Cartland in 1978 sang an Album of Love Songs with the Royal Philharmonic Orchestra.

In private life Barbara Cartland, who is a Dame of the Order of St. John of Jerusalem, Chairman of the St. John Council in Hertfordshire and Deputy President of the St. John Ambulance Brigade, has fought for better conditions and salaries for Midwives and Nurses.

She championed the cause for the Elderly in 1956 invoking a Government Enquiry into the "Housing Conditions of Old People."

In 1962 she had the Law of England changed so that Local Authorities had to provide camps for their own Gypsies. This has meant that since then thousands and thousands of Gypsy children have been able to go to School, which they had never been able to do in the past, as their caravans were moved every twenty-four hours by the Police.

There are now fourteen camps in Hertfordshire and Barbara Cartland has her own Romany Gypsy Camp called Barbaraville by the Gypsies.

Her designs "Decorating with Love" are being sold all over the U.S.A. and the National Home Fashions League made her, in 1981, "Woman of Achievement."

She is unique in that she was one and two in the Dalton list of Best Sellers, and one week had four books in the top twenty.

Barbara Cartland's book *Getting Older, Growing Younger* has been published in Great Britain and the

U.S.A. and her fifth cookery book, *The Romance of Food*, is now being used by the House of Commons.

In 1984 she received at Kennedy Airport America's Bishop Wright Industry Award for her contribution to the development of aviation. In 1931, she and two R.A.F. Officers thought of, and carried, the first aeroplane-towed glider air-mail.

During the War she was Chief Lady Welfare Officer in Bedfordshire looking after 20,000 Service men and women. She thought of having a pool of Wedding Dresses at the War Office so a Service Bride could hire a gown for the day.

She bought 1000 gowns without coupons for the A.T.S., the W.A.A.F.'s and the W.R.E.N.S. In 1945 Barbara Cartland received the Certificate of Merit from Eastern Command.

In 1964 Barbara Cartland founded the National Association for Health of which she is the President, as a front for all the Health Stores and for any product made as alternative medicine.

This is now a £300,000 turnover a year, with one third going in export.

In January 1988 she received "La Médaille de Vermeil de la Ville de Paris." This is the highest award to be given in France by the City of Paris for achievement. She had sold 25 million books in France.